BEFORE TIMES

BY SAM

MAULDIN

ISBN: 9798300429577 First Edition

Any references to historical events, real people, or real places are used fictitiously. Names, characters, and places are products of the author's imagination.

Front cover image by Sam Mauldin.

Book design by Sam Mauldin.

Edited by Mara Birkerts

Published by Kajam Publishing LLC, in the United States of America

First printing edition 2024.

2013 Valle Vista St, Santa Fe, NM 87505

FOR MARA…

An old woman approaches you on the street, with a book. She says: "Here! Take this. It's called *Before Times*, by some guy named Sam Mauldin. It's fourteen short stories. They're *wild*. Living drugs, undead feral hogs, haunted movie theaters, rats, and more. Take it!"

Will you accept her gift?

TABLE OF CONTENTS:

EMERALD ---
------------------------ 7

HOGRA THE TERRIBLE --
------------------------ 15

THE SNOW GLOBE BLOCK --
------------------------ 83

STAFF ONLY --
------------------------ 99

TRASH PANDA ---
------------------------ 123

THE MECHANICAL AMERICAN -----------------------------------
------------------------ 131

ORANGIE AND THE GATES ---
------------------------ 162

WHERE DO THEY GO? --
------------------------ 176

FAMOUS GREMLINS ---
------------------------ 189

LAZDA --
------------------------ 205

THE DAM --
---------------------- 232

BIRD DANIELS --
---------------------- 276

THE WALK-IN --
---------------------- 290

MARK ---
---------------------- 315

ACKNOWLEDGEMENTS ---
---------------------- 341

EMERALD

A lamp flickers. Todd shuffles on his couch. Was he sleeping? Maybe. His living room is dark, and dirty. Greasy pizza boxes, empty beer cans, among other horrors. He itches his crotch.

"DOES THIS *LIKE FUN TO YOU?"*

The TV is yelling. There's a vacant-eyed couple on the screen. They're also sitting on a sofa. It's like looking into a mirror. But they have angry red sores, all over their arms. Purple, leaking boils. Dark scabs. Ominous music thuds. They start spasming. The narrator goes on.

"EMERALD'S SIDE EFFECTS INCLUDE…"

Strobe lights flash. The TV couple is frothing at the mouth. Todd shrugs. At least this PSA is pretty metal. Are those chips finally kicking in? Matilda groans, next to him. Todd turns down the TV, and looks at his wife. Her body is glistening. Soaked with cold sweat. Damn. Did they take too much? They say that emerald packs a punch, and it's their first time trying it.

"How do I look?"

That smoky voice. Matilda's blue eyes have a deep, probing curiosity, even when they're bloodshot and glassy. She's studying Todd. He says the first thing that comes to his head.

"You actually look *great*, babe."

That was probably a mistake, but Todd winks. He couldn't help it. Matilda scowls back.

"*IT WAS THEIR FIRST TIME TRYING EMERALD…*"

Todd jumps. What the fuck? The TV got louder, but he turned it down. Didn't he?

"*…AND THEIR LAST!*"

He gulps. Is it watching *them*? Damn. Maybe taking two chips was a bad call. Todd's heard many horror stories about emerald, "*The Living Drug That's Killing Americans.*"

Matilda gave him two opaque, neon green capsules an hour ago. He's nervous. Emerald is made with something more potent than chemicals. Every pill contains a chip. It's a *smart drug*: an AI program. It bonds with its host. It stimulates pleasure and euphoria, in a custom way, to meet the demands of its users. To give them things they didn't even know they wanted. They say it lasts for days. That nothing feels better. He's about to find out. Matilda clears her throat.

"I feel like I'm gonna fucking faint."

Shit. Todd shakes his head. He grabs a glass from the coffee table.

"Here, have some water."

And hopes that it's actually water. Matilda takes the sweating glass with dancing ice cubes. She drinks it down like she needs ten more, but her eyelids are falling. Todd gulps. What will happen if she faints? What the hell is he supposed to do? Should he keep Matilda awake, like she got a concussion? Should he let her sleep? Which one? Neither of them? Fuck. He yells.

"*Babe*! What am I supposed to do if you faint?!?"

Matilda frowns, like she just smelled some shit.

"What…are you…talking about?"

Her voice is groggy. Distant, fading fast. Sweat runs down Todd's forehead. He asks.

"Am I supposed to wake you up? Let you rest? What?!"

Matilda nods, with her eyes half-open. Panic is knocking. These are important questions, that Todd should know. He's married. An *adult*.

But all he remembers is a rant from a bar.

A wasted nurse was talking about emerald. She had odd, olive green eyes.

There was a square tattoo on her temple, tucked near her hairline. It looked like a computer chip. He expected gruesome, cautionary tales, but she praised the drug. *"It's like old quaaludes, mixed with heavy, synthetic psychedelics…"* She went on about toad sweat, and branding. The nurse talked like a saleswoman. Todd was hooked. An animalistic attraction was growing between them, but he also felt like prey. He asked if emerald could refuse to let go of a brain. The nurse frowned. *"Never, and I mean never, let someone faint on that shit."* He asked *why*, but someone bumped into him, spilling his beer. When he looked up, the nurse was gone.

Todd told Matilda about *most* of it, the next day. Her reply shocked him. She had already scored four emerald chips, and wanted to try it. Now Matilda's eyes are flickering, like the lamp.

Todd blinks. The couch turned green. It's growing. The coffee table drips. Wood legs sprout hairs. Sharp claws flex, at the end of its toes. Shit. He feels great. A wave is crashing over. It's joy, but a little bit more. Fuck. He's about to be engulfed by a powerful drug that he's never done, and his wife is already in too deep. He needs to pull her out, before he goes in. Todd yells.

"*Babe*! Wake up! You gotta stay with me!"

"What…are you…talking about?"

Matilda is whispering, but still holding on. Todd stammers.

"That nurse warned me, *never let someone faint on emerald*!"

His wife nods, after five seconds. As if she agreed to something else. Leaves, branches, and trunks burst through Todd's living room walls. They snap, and groan. He sees spirals in the bark. There isn't much time, before the emerald swallows him. A jungle is calling.

"Oh, *you know*. They wake up with a…"

Matilda mumbles the rest. Shit. What is she talking about? Those muffled syllables could've been important. Todd asks.

"With *what*, Matilda?! What do they wake up with?"

Something strong and irresistible is pulling her under. Matilda whispers.

"They wake up with a…"

Then buries the last part of her riddle in a murmur, again. She shuts her eyes. Fuck. She's a *heavy* sleeper. They have a fleet of alarm clocks, and need a hundred more. Even a marching band would have trouble with his wife, but Todd has to try. He shakes her, hard.

"WITH *WHAT,* MATILDA!? *WHAT DO THEY WAKE UP WITH*?!?"

Eyelids snap open. Matilda bolts up, like a startled cat, and glares at Todd. Damn. That worked, a little too well. Now she's *wired*, but something else changed. It's basic, fundamental.

A spark is gone. Her eyes had wonder. Deep, probing curiosity, and a cynical, silly joy. Now, those same windows into her soul reveal far simpler thoughts. They're empty. Angry. All laughter is gone. So is their glacial blue shade. Todd blinks. Matilda's eyes turned green.

What the fuck? This isn't his wife. Those eyes belong to another person, but they seem familiar. Todd gulps. His wife doesn't have tattoos, but there's ink on this woman's temple, by her hairline. It's square. A computer chip. Fuck. That nurse also had olive green eyes. Did she possess Matilda? Or did someone else trap them both? Or some*thing*. Will Todd ever know if this *living* drug has let go of his mind? He looks up. The forest is gone. Circuits replaced it. Wires, blinking lights. Endless mainframes. The TV vanished, but it's everywhere. So are the patterns, but these new ones are rigid, uniform. Is the drug *adjusting*, or showing its true colors?

He backs away from the woman on the sofa, but burning green emeralds stay focused on Todd. She smiles. She seems to *sense* his fear. She likes it. Not-Matilda finally speaks.

"They wake up quickly."

HOGRA THE

TERRIBLE

Hot dust is blowing across Bubba's airfield. The wind was already fast and mean before the chopper arrived. Its departure isn't helping. Bubba coughs and looks at his dream. It's a long, cracked line of pavement. Decorated like a junkyard and surrounded by dirt. Baby dunes growing around his sheds are laying down roots, like those predatory vines that strangle trees, in lands blessed with more rain. One bad storm could bury it all, but Bubba loves his airfield. It's peaceful. An island of freedom, where he can pause to reflect. But the peace never lasts long.

He stares at the famous ruined helicopter. It's a sculpture, of sorts. Deep, running gashes are carved all over its twisted, metallic body. But for Bubba, this big, expensive wreck doesn't represent a financial loss. No, it's become a *magnet* for money, and a crucial piece of evidence. It's proof of his close encounter. It screams: The rumors are true. Hogra the Terrible is back.

Something cold and furry is rubbing against Bubba's sand-blasted jeans. It's Bernie.

Years ago, Bubba found this strange grey cat in a ditch. Bernie is evasive, a shadow. He carries a bizarre, pungent, earthy odor. And he's smart. Real smart. Bernie's bond with Bubba is strong. They speak two different languages, but understand each other. And now the stinky cat with yellow lantern eyes is telling his hunting partner to focus.

Bubba hears laughter. Up ahead, shapes that resemble people emerge from a wall of dust. It's today's clients. Bubba is a hunting guide. He takes rich people out to the badlands, to kill wild boars. Business was slow, up until he lived through the story behind the wrecked helicopter.

Now lots of people want to hunt with Bubba. They want the big prize, the legend.

They want to kill the thing that he saw, the thing that shouldn't exist.

Hogra the Terrible became famous after he died. A hunter shot the wild boar, and a photo of Hogra's twelve foot long, thousand-pound carcass went viral. He set records. The world had never seen such a massive feral pig before. Hogra had cow-spotted black and white fur, and a distinct dark spot on his hide, shaped like the state of Maine. Many cheered his demise. But now, somehow, Hogra is back. Whispers of his return were mocked, until the hunter who shot him vanished, and was never found. Rumors grew shrill, and took on supernatural dimensions.

And Bubba is the only person who has ever seen this resurrected beast, and lived.

Hogra got larger since he went viral. His tusks got sharper. And he got a lot meaner too.

News and fact checking sites say Bubba faked their whole encounter for publicity. They assure the gullible: Hogra the Terrible is still dead. But Bubba knows what he saw, and official denunciations only made his business boom. He has a waiting list now. He gets to be *selective*.

He can charge the kind of prices that are meant for people who don't care about prices.

Like these four assholes. They have beards, camouflage outfits, long rifles and tactical luggage. It's all expensive, brand new. They want to look tough. But costumes don't fool Bubba.

The four beards are swatting at the dust storm. They don't want their rugged gear to get dirty.

They won't like it here. In a dusty, arid landscape like this, cleanliness as these brats know it is a mirage, an impossible oasis that will drive the sane to madness in its endless pursuit.

They're still laughing. At the rumors? At Bubba? Maybe both.

He lets his new clients laugh.

They won't be laughing when they're out hunting in the Nowhere Woods.

They won't be laughing when they enter the circle of soil, and see Hogra the Terrible.

And when they see what Bubba and Bernie are up to, they won't think it's funny either.

These four beards think they're anonymous. They paid in cash and used fake names, but Bubba knows who they are. He did his homework. He thinks about the old photo album with a worn spine, the one that's hidden under the driver's seat in his truck. It needs some new editions.

The beards are close now. A big man at the head of the pack walks up to Bubba and says.

"The name's Roy. You must be Bubba. We're here to kill Hogra the Terrible."

Roy is tall and built like a bull. His head is shaped like an angry brick. A wide, fraudulent smile shows off teeth that are far too white. His blue eyes are empty and busy. They shake hands. Roy's grip is strong, but squishy. After they let go, Roy rubs his palms together, like a greedy tycoon. Maybe he's trying to cleanse them, after touching something foul. Bubba chooses to be amused instead of offended, but Bernie growls. Bubba thinks: *just be patient*, then replies.

"You're not the first person who's said that, Roy."

"Oh, I'm aware, Bubba. But you've never guided a crew like mine before."

Three bearded yes-men scowl behind Roy. Bubba knows two of them. Who's the new guy? The fourth beard is tall and skinny. His red hat has an American flag. Is he a banker? An oil man? Did he flee his bland McMansion and timid servants, for an adventure? He isn't wearing trophies like the others. Is this their initiation rite? Bubba knows the other two short, husky yes-men. Their matching black hats have bold white letters. *WE THE PEOPLE*. Which ones?

"There's a lot of wrecks out here. What's wrong with your airfield, Bubba? Is it *cursed*?"

Roy's yes-men chuckle behind their master. Bubba shrugs and replies.

"Shit tends to break out here. The dust isn't kind to expensive, delicate things."

The four beards get quiet. Did that go over their heads? Probably. Bubba keeps talking.

"But you're referring to a *very* specific wreck, aren't you? Why wait?"

He starts walking towards the sculpture. The four beards follow Bubba, whispering.

"You really think it's fake?"

"It has to be."

"This airfield is a dump, and that guy needs *something*, to lure people out here."

"Besides, zombies aren't fucking real!"

But when they get close to the wreckage, they shut up. Up close, they see that one man with blowtorches, saws and hammers couldn't have staged, or faked this jagged nightmare.

Bubba stares at the wrecked helicopter too. Flashes of terror rip through his mind. He was trapped in there for hours. He watched Hogra the Terrible make every gash in the chopper's steel body. Bubba and Hogra got to know each other well. Too well. The four beards mutter.

"Whoa..."

"How the fuck..."

Roy knocks on the chopper. Hollow, metallic clangs rattle across the shredded wreck. Did he think it was fake metal? Probably, but not anymore. His yes-men go on.

"Those tusks, man..."

"If they can cut through steel like that, imagine..."

The husky beard doesn't finish his thought. The four men shiver in the dust storm. They don't want to imagine the horrors that Bubba saw, yet they paid a lot of money to come out here and follow him into the woods where he saw them. Their eagerness is loud. So is their bloodlust.

Bubba hears pained squawking below. He looks down. Bernie just caught another bird. The blue jay is flapping its wings and crying for mercy. Why the hell was it flying in this storm? Bad move. Now it's pinned below the cat's matted grey paw. And yet Bernie isn't triumphant. He's tense, sticking close to Bubba. Bernie doesn't like these new clients. One of them asks.

"Why don't we just go out and hunt Hogra in a giant fucking APC?"

Bubba keeps staring at the wreck, but he imagines a tank with no cannon trying to cross the Nowhere Woods. He wants to laugh, but Bubba shakes his head, clicks his tongue and says.

"Not a chance. Hogra will hear that giant, loud-ass engine coming from *miles* away. Wild boars are smart as hell, but Hogra the Terrible is smarter. An Einstein among fellow physicists. He's a master of hiding. No, he won't appear unless *we* come to *him*, on foot."

The four beards look at each other in silence. They're on edge, so Bubba pushes them.

"What? Are you boys *scared* of going out in the field and facing Hogra on your own?"

Four tempers boil over. One of the stocky beards shouts.

"FUCK YOU!"

He charges at Bubba, but someone snatches him by the shoulder, fast. It's Roy. He yells.

"*Enough*, Zeke! Apologize to Bubba! This man is a *legend* around here!"

Bubba ignores flattery. Roy hates him too. The alpha beard is just being diplomatic. He's smarter than his yes-men, and knows who holds the key to his prize. Guys like him only defend guys like Bubba if they're desperate. Roy doesn't just want to kill Hogra. He *needs* to. Why is he so obsessed with slaying the biggest, scariest animal of all? To prove something? Zeke sighs.

"Sorry, Bubba."

He isn't, not really. Zeke's only apologizing because he's afraid of Roy. Bubba replies.

"It's okay, Zeke. I have thick skin. You have to, to survive out here."

That didn't go over their heads. Roy sees the anger rising in his yes-men, so he shouts.

"Zeke, Phil, Rex! Load up your gear into the truck! I wanna be ready to roll in five!"

They start hauling their tactical luggage towards Bubba's truck. Cameras? Why not? Roy is already talking about the truck like it's his. Bubba doesn't mind. He looks at the sky and says.

"We better hurry up. The sun is setting in an hour. Hogra likes to hunt at night."

But Roy doesn't move. He's still staring at the deep, long gashes in the chopper. He says.

"Sorry about that guy, Bubba. He won a contest at the office, to come out with us today."

Roy chuckles. He also just lied. Zeke always hunts with Roy. Bubba knows this, just like he knows when a client isn't being serious about dangerous things. Bubba narrows his eyes.

"Do you want to die today?"

Roy's fake, hospitable grin is erased by shock. An honest scowl replaces it. He exclaims.

"Of course not! My life is..."

"Good. I don't give a fuck who they are, Roy. I don't care who you are either. Just know this. Out there, *I'm* in charge. We're not just hunting a wild, dangerous animal. Hogra is a force of nature. A creature strong and stubborn enough to cheat death. Normal feral hogs are smart as dolphins, but Hogra is on a whole other level. So do what I say, or you might get us *all* killed."

Roy nods, then smirks. Why? Bubba didn't tell any jokes. Maybe Roy doesn't think Hogra actually came back from the dead, even if the rumors are why he's here. Bubba adds.

"Those guys listen to you. Tell them who's in charge out here. But pull them aside first. *Something* tells me that they won't be very happy, when they get the news."

Roy turns around. His yes-men stopped loading up their gear, when he wasn't looking. Now they're crowded around Zeke, laughing at something on his phone. How are they getting the internet out here? Bubba shivers. Its tentacles get longer every day. Roy yells.

"*HEY*! You fucking idiots! Listen up!"

The yes-men get pale. Zeke drops his phone. He should've enjoyed the internet while it lasted. Out in the

Nowhere Woods, there's no service. No people, no nothing. Just the mercy of nature, and a giant, feral hog who shouldn't be alive. Roy walks over and delivers the bad news.

"Are you fucking serious!?"

Bubba tunes out the yes-men's next, predictable groans, until Roy interrupts them.

"What do you idiots think this is, a safari? We're hunting *Hogra*! He's smarter than a fucking dolphin! Besides, y'all remember the waiver that you signed before we left, don't you?"

Roy's question silences his yes-men. His grin gets more sadistic, and honest. He goes on.

"If anything happens to you out here, I'm not liable. You know what that means, *Phil*?"

The new guy nods. He must be Phil. Unlike the other three, Phil isn't wearing a trophy made from an endangered animal. At least, not that Bubba can see. Phil isn't part of their club. Zeke has his snake boots. Rex has his frog skin belt. And Roy has his ring. He keeps talking.

"Good. I don't care about your lives. I care about *mine*. And if you fucking idiots disobey Bubba out there, it could get *me* killed. And *I* don't want to die today. Do you, Phil?"

"No, boss."

"How about you, Zeke?"

"No, *sir*!"

"That's more like it! Alright, now finish loading up your shit, and get ready to move!"

The yes-men turn to their tasks. They hate Bubba, but listen to Roy. But how long can he give up control? That fraudulent smile is holding, but Roy isn't strong enough keep it up forever. He's being cooperative now, but will he drop the act, once they get out to the Nowhere Woods?

Bubba looks down. Bernie killed the blue jay while the giants were talking. *Dissected* might be a better way to describe it. The strange cat is staring at Bubba, but he can't stop staring at the dead bird. Dust from the storm is already building up around the crime scene and burying it, but Bubba sees what Bernie did. The pattern that he made with the blue jay's blood.

It's a spiral.

Twenty minutes later, Bubba is driving down a long, dirt road in his pick-up truck.

The dusty interior is full of memories. Roy is sitting shotgun. His three idiots are in the back of the truck. Bubba used to love riding back there when he was a kid, but these yes-men clearly grew up with valets. They're bouncing around back there with their guns and tactical luggage, like dimes in a shaking can. It's a rough road, and a new mosh pit starts every time Bubba hits a bump. Somehow, he hasn't missed one yet. He opens a sliding window behind his seat. It's a portal to the back of the truck. It gets loud and dusty fast. Bubba shouts over the wind.

"You boys doing ok back there?!"

"NO!!"

"How much longer?"

"I don't have any service!"

Bubba smiles at their complaints and yells through the rear sliding window.

"Happy you boys are doing good! I'll try not to swerve too much!"

Then shuts it. It gets quiet in the truck. Roy looks like he wants to talk business.

"What's up with the cat?"

Bubba looks down. He almost forgot that Bernie is sitting in his lap. He replies.

"Bernie is my hunting partner. Wherever I go, he goes."

Roy sniffs, cringes from Bernie's earthy smell, rolls down his window and says.

"Don't those things bathe themselves?"

The strange cat glares at Roy. Bernie's deeply offended. He holds grudges. Bubba laughs.

"Out here? Why bother?"

A gust of wind and grit hits his truck like a firehose, right on cue. Roy coughs, then asks.

"But *why* does the cat go wherever you go?"

"Because the one time that Bernie didn't come hunting with me, Hogra attacked me."

Bubba turns to the angry brick riding shotgun. Shit. He forgot to move the pictures. They're still stashed in the sun visor, right above Roy. That big, blazing orb is sitting low on the horizon. Soon its glare will be blasting directly ahead of them. It'll be piercing. And if Roy pulls the sun visor down, those pictures will fall on his lap. That can't happen. It'll spoil the surprise. Bernie grunts like a big insect. He tells Bubba to distract Roy, fast. Luckily, they were already talking about Hogra the Terrible. Roy can't resist. He asks.

"So, what was *he* like?"

Bubba smiles.

"Who, the Pope?"

"No, Bubba. You *know* who I'm talking about."

Roy is like a kid who's waiting to hear a new rumor about Santa Claus. Bubba says.

"Hogra was wider than this truck. Taller too. His tusks were bigger than my forearm. But he was sneaky. Quiet too. And *fast.* When he charged at me, I opened fire with my deer rifle, but I might as well have used BBs. I shot him four times. In the head. But Hogra never broke pace."

Bubba exhales. He left out a lot. Hogra's yellow eyes. His snout, the way it moved like a sucker under a squid's tentacle. And the bugs. The fucking bugs. Roy shifts in his seat, like a kid at a sleepover who realizes that his friends chose a movie that's way too scary. He wants to call his mom. The ride started, but he wants to jump off now, before it's too late. Good. Roy asks.

"But the rumors aren't true, right?"

"What are you talking about, Roy? What rumors?"

"*You know.* They say that Hogra is undead. A zombie. But that's all bullshit, right?"

Roy looks hopeful, even gullible. How cute. Bubba shrugs and says.

"Don't you want to know how I survived?"

Roy blinks. He's confused. Bubba hits a rut, ignores the three whining yes-men and adds.

"I just told you that I put four bullets in Hogra's head while he was charging at me, but he never broke pace. Don't you want to know what happened next, Roy? How I'm still alive?"

"No. You're here. End of story. Just tell me. Is Hogra the Terrible a zombie, or not?"

Roy glares, letting his caged hate pound on the jail bars that were just put up behind his glacial blue eyes. This angry brick wolf isn't even trying to dress up like grandma. Bubba says.

"I don't spend time putting labels on things. I just accept them as they are. Was that pig a zombie? Was he actually Hogra? I didn't ask while he was attacking me, but the big bastard certainly *looked* like the hog in that famous photo. Hell, he even had a dark spot on his hide, shaped like Maine. But don't worry, Roy. If Hogra comes out tonight, you can ID him yourself."

Bubba expects laughter, or an explosion of rage, but instead, Roy just looks down at the shiny new assault rifle on his lap. The angry brick pats the gun like a loyal dog, and says.

"Oh *I will,* Bubba. I will. We'll have plenty of time for questions, after I put Hogra down. Luckily, this baby is much stronger than your deer rifle. She's automatic, loaded with hollow-tip, armor-piercing rounds. Hogra the Terrible will get *a lot* more than four shots, from me."

Roy's arrogance is almost amusing. He truly thinks he's better than everyone else, and that any unsolved problem is only unsolved, because he hasn't tried to solve it yet. He adds.

"But tell me, Bubba. Now I'm curious. How *did* you survive?"

"I got lucky. I jumped in the helicopter and shut the door, before Hogra got to me. He rammed his head into my makeshift cage, over and over. He shook it like a toy, and carved it up with his tusks. I was trapped in that chopper, watching him try to kill me, for a *long* damn time. Hours passed. Maybe years. Eventually, a deer ran by. Hogra chased after it, and he was gone."

Bubba tries to hide it, but he can't. He shivers. That wasn't the whole story, of course.

Roy will hear the rest later. He almost looks impressed, but arrogance can't help itself.

"Why didn't you shoot Hogra again? Did you only have four shots left in your rifle?"

"No, Roy. I had plenty of ammo."

"Well, then why didn't you shoot Hogra again, Bubba!? *I* would've!"

"You ever hunted a feral hog before?"

"No, but I've shot plenty of other…"

"Oh I know, Roy. *I know.*"

The angry brick frowns. Roy hates getting interrupted. He doesn't like *I know*, or its subtle implications either. Good. Bubba knows what he really does for work, and why he didn't use his real name. Roy is a poacher. Endangered animals are his trade. He's personally driven several species all the way to extinction. Bubba can see it now, on the ring that Roy is wearing. It looks simple, even humble, but it's made out of rhino horn. Their natural protection became a curse, after rhino horns became more valuable than gold. Roy probably got that ring when he finished one of the last ones off. Fuck him, but this silence is dangerous. Bubba keeps talking.

"But feral hogs are different. They're faster than you think, and smarter too. I know a guy who catches them. He has to keep building new traps, because the hogs keep learning how to break out of them. They pile up on top of each other, to build living exit ramps. They work as a team, to escape. And those are just regular hogs. Remember, Hogra is a genius among them."

"Now wait a minute, Bubba! How the hell can pigs be *that* smart?"

"*Never* underestimate feral pigs, even if it isn't Hogra. They have no natural predators, just us. You can't sue them, or scare them. If they want to get you, they will. They can run thirty miles an hour. They can smell prey from five miles away. I don't even think of them as animals when I hunt them. They're more like stealthy meth-heads, with machetes and riot armor."

It gets quiet in the truck. Bubba's truck hits another bump in the rough road, setting off a new chorus of moans from the yes-men riding in the back. Roy says.

"I *never* underestimate my enemies, Bubba."

He's glaring. Roy's last comment was dripping with menace, so Bubba smiles back.

"Good. That means that you want to live."

The quiet resumes. The angry brick is trying to scare Bubba, but compared to the things he's seen in the Nowhere Woods, Roy and his gun are gnats. But this silence can't linger much longer, or Roy might fuck around with the sun visor, so Bubba keeps talking.

"What were you saying earlier, about the three amigos back there? They won a prize?"

Bernie tenses up on Bubba's lap. The strange cat is listening close. Roy furrows his brow.

"I thought you didn't give a fuck about them, Bubba?"

He's an arrogant brute, but Roy is sharp. Yet his needs and his bloodlust are making him miss key details. Bernie growls, and a thought pops into Bubba's mind. *Keep it simple.* He says.

"It's a long ride, Roy. I'm bored."

Roy frowns, but he seems bored too. He turns to the rear sliding portal and says.

"You see the tall, skinny guy? That's Phil. He's the best shot in my whole company. We have marksmanship contests at the shooting range for holiday parties, and Phil can shoot a flea off a rhino's head, from three hundred yards. And the other two idiots are my camera crew."

Roy's ring says he knows about shooting at rhinos. Does he think Bubba knows? Maybe. The angry brick is suspicious, but his curiosity is way too strong to let him turn back now. Bubba stares at Phil. Is he a good shot? He's clearly the new guy. He's the only one who isn't wearing a trophy from an endangered animal. Does Phil know what the others do? Is this his initiation rite? Or maybe he really did win a prize. If so, Phil might be one of history's unluckiest winners.

Bernie relaxes, slightly. Why? Then Bubba looks at the road ahead. Shit. Looking out of the windshield is painful now. The sun is low. Roy might use his sun visor soon, so Bubba yells.

"Your camera crew?! You didn't mention *that*, when you booked this fucking trip!"

He isn't really mad. Roy even mentioned them earlier, but he says.

"What's wrong with that, Bubba? You don't like having your picture taken?"

The truck gets quiet. *This is too easy*. Bubba growls.

"Wow, Roy. That's a *real* vintage stereotype, right there! A collector's item! You better check the date on that one and look it up, it might be worth a lot!"

Roy's face contorts. Will he scream, or get self-defensive? Bubba keeps talking.

"And despite what you *think* you know about me, I know what a fucking camera crew does. And they're a pain in the ass. They have to set up shots. It takes time. It makes noise. Fuck that. We're here to shoot Hogra the Terrible, not a movie. If we don't take a shot, because *their* shot isn't just right, we'll die out there. Don't forget, Roy. Hogs can sneak up on us, too."

Bernie is buzzing in Bubba's lap. The stinky grey cat agrees, he just would've used a lot less words. Roy nods, but his calm mask is slipping. Veins bulge in his swollen neck. He says.

"I'll keep those idiots in line. You're the boss out there, Bubba. I haven't forgotten."

Roy's voice was low, a controlled release. But he smiles. He's really straining himself for this performance. Bubba hits another bump on the road. Three yes-men bounce around in the cab of his truck. Back there, with their beards, machine guns and body armor, they look like cheap American knock-offs of insurgents. Bubba can't trust any of them. Their grandparents would've told them to shoot him where he stood if he even dared to talk back to them, and they know it.

Bubba has to watch out. At least Hogra the Terrible had the decency to be loud when he snuck up on Bubba. The four beards won't be so polite.

Twenty minutes later, Bubba parks at the edge of a ridge. The sun is low on the horizon. Soon, it'll start glowing red. The sky will turn purple, going on black. When it does, Bubba will warn them, one last time. He gets out of the truck. So does Roy.

Bubba smiles at a thin stream below. It's a miracle that cuts through the barren landscape, leaving a green trail of trees and bushes in its wake. But this ridge is far from the miracle stream. The creosote bushes next to him are dry. This drought has lasted too long. It might be permanent.

This soil is thirsty. So are the animals, hiding all around them. Everything out here is fighting for survival, except the four rich jerks that Bubba is escorting into their parched world. He needs a new job. But when Bernie hops out of the truck and rolls around in the dirt, chortling like a madman who swallowed a bird, Bubba remembers why he's so selective.

Then he sees a dense pack of trees up ahead. Oh yes. They lead into the Nowhere Woods.

Green leaves hide dry, brittle trunks. If that bark could talk...

Three yes-men get out of the back of the truck, real slow. They must feel great after that bumpy trip across the badlands. But they aren't stretching. They're smacking their phones.

"No fucking signal! Do you have service?"

"Not a bar, nothing! Rex! Do..."

"SHUT THE FUCK UP!"

Roy's yes-men get quiet and pale. He keeps talking.

"Y'all remember the wrecked helicopter from Bubba's airfield? The one that looked like it got mauled by a goddamn T-Rex? Well, while you assholes were complaining back there, I heard what happened. Bubba shot Hogra The Terrible in the head, *four times*, and that pig kept coming! Bubba hid in that chopper. Hogra tried to get him in there, for hours. So, remember that wreck. If Hogra could do that to a fucking helicopter, what do you think he can do to *you*?"

The yes-men get quiet. For a precious few seconds, the miracle stream below is the only thing that Bubba can hear. It's beautiful. But then Phil, the office marksman, finally pipes up.

"If you were hunting Hogra in your chopper, why was it grounded when he attacked?"

Phil is the only yes-man who's asking smart questions, or talking to Bubba like a person. He's the new guy, the only question mark. But Bubba won't get too excited about Phil. He says.

"I wasn't hunting Hogra that day, I didn't even believe the rumors about his resurrection. I was just flying another tourist, like y'all, to hunt feral hogs. We both needed to take a piss, so I landed. But he walked deeper into the woods than I did. That's when Hogra snuck up on us."

Wind blows across the ridge, almost as if it came from the Nowhere Woods themselves. Bubba hears a strange animal call, coming from deep within those trees. Roy frowns, then says.

"You didn't mention that there was another person with you earlier, Bubba."

New wrinkles and trenches appear on the angry brick's forehead. Roy is right. Bubba did omit many details when he told this story to Roy, but on this ridge, at the edge of the

Nowhere Woods, they hit different. Bubba won't answer Roy's question yet. He just waits, until Phil asks.

"What happened to him?"

"I heard him scream. Then his body flew out of the trees, like a ragdoll. And then I saw Hogra. I shot him in the head four times, then ran into the chopper. He was fast, strong and way too smart. He tore up that chopper for hours. After Hogra the Terrible finally left, I tried to find the tourist's body, but he was gone. Search parties went out, but it was all a formality. We knew where his body wound up. But that's digestion for you. It leaves no evidence."

Three beards look down and shuffle. They're getting nervous. But not Roy. He yells.

"*HEY*, Bubba! Why didn't you say that someone died while you were *guiding* them!?"

How cute. The angry brick is masking his terror with chest-thumping. Bubba replies.

"You didn't ask, Roy. I warned that tourist not to go too far into these woods, but he didn't listen. Back then, I let clients like you disrespect me. I wanted to be a people pleaser. I didn't want to get a bad review online. So I let that guy walk all over me, and it got him killed."

Bubba pauses to look over the four scowling beards, one by one, before he continues.

"I've never made that same mistake again, and no one else has died under my watch. So, when I give you guys orders out there in the Nowhere Woods, you better fucking listen. Got it?"

They nod. Roy even smiles. He's lying through his shiny white teeth. Then Phil asks.

"Wait…Hogra killed that guy, in *these* woods? At this exact same spot?!"

Bubba shows the four beards his genuine smile for the very first time.

"That's why we're here, isn't it?"

He turns away from them and starts walking towards the dense cluster of trees.

The four beards hoist up their tripods and follow Bubba into the Nowhere Woods.

Thirty minutes later, they're resting next to a stream, and surrounded by trees. It's dark. The wind is calm, cool. Bubba won't look at the trees for long, or the shadows around them. Pale bark from their trunks is glowing all around, like spectral spires. Bubba knows what's out there, so he's staring at Bernie, listening. The stream isn't in a hurry. Neither are the four beards. They didn't ask to stop. Rex collapsed, from thirst. The idiot didn't bring any water. Without his maid, he probably didn't even know that he had to drink water. The other yes-men dragged him to this stream, and Rex is still chugging water like he just discovered it. Phil is cleaning his long rifle. It's mounted on a tripod, with a scope. Of course he's a good shot. With that set-up, anyone could be. Zeke is setting up a camera. Then Bubba turns to Roy. The angry brick is cleaning his rifle too, but it doesn't look like he has an undead feral hog in mind. He's staring at Bubba.

Is Roy thinking about the words *I know*? Is he wondering *what* Bubba knows? Good.

Bernie is buzzing in Bubba's lap. He pets the cat's knotted head. Then Phil says.

"Hey, Bubba. I'm sorry, but you saw Hogra the Terrible up close, so I have to ask. Is it true? Did the big bastard actually die and come back to life? Is he really a zombie feral hog?"

Bubba thinks about Hogra's yellow eyes. Their dull, lantern-like glimmer. The sulphur, the bullet holes, the bugs. He should tell Phil to fuck off, but Bubba says nothing. He lets the question linger in the air. A running stream and howling crickets decorate it. Phil is the winner, the new guy. The only question mark out here. And he finally brought up the whole *undead* part of Hogra's legend. It's why these four beards came here, but they don't want to talk about it.

Then Bernie's back stiffens. Uh-oh. A twig snaps.

Bubba tenses up. The noise was close by. Real close. Something is out there.

Phil aims his rifle, hits buttons and leans into the scope. Thermal vision? Another cheat code? Bubba waits, then relaxes. Whatever snapped that twig left in a hurry. Zeke shouts.

"Dammit! We missed it!"

Bubba smirks, until he hears another noise, somewhere from the depths of those pale, glowing spires. It sounds like a dying bird, but it isn't. He's heard this call before, but only here, in the Nowhere Woods. It's a reminder. He has to give them one more warning. Bubba says.

"I don't like this. We should get out of here and come back tomorrow."

The yes-men blink. A finger jabs Bubba's chest. It's Roy. He's fast, and quiet. He says.

"Let's get one thing clear, Bubba. We're not going back with nothing. No way. I don't give a fuck if we have to stay out here all night, or through the next goddamn day! GOT IT?!?"

Bubba is surprised the angry brick obeyed his authority for thirty whole minutes. He says.

"Fine by me, Roy. My meter is running, and you're the one paying. But if you want to catch Hogra the Terrible, we can't stay here. We're gonna have to keep moving."

Roy nods. Money truly means nothing to him, unless someone who needs it is asking.

They walk deeper into the Nowhere Woods. The trees get denser. The crickets got drunk and found megaphones. Any signs of humanity are long gone. Darkness is spreading. Time passes by, fast and slow at the same time. It's like they've always been out here, but it also feels like they just arrived. The sun went down at some point, and got replaced by the moon.

That thin, dim crescent above is making the Nowhere Woods even darker than normal. Bubba listens and keeps walking deeper. It's usually loud in here. Not now. Other than crickets, wind gusts and a distant stream, the woods are quiet. But they aren't deserted. They're on edge.

The strange, stinky cat walks next to Bubba. Bernie's fur looks like porcupine needles. His eyes are low and alert, like a city dweller minding his business. Bubba knows why. He and his friend are both curious beings, but out here, many things are best left unknown. Neither will look at the tree trunks for long. They know what they'll find, if they stare. And their faces will spoil the surprise. But the beards aren't paying attention. Their bloodlust is running too deep.

Time passes, fast and slow at the same time. Eventually, they stop by a clearing.

It's a circle of soil, where the densely packed trees abruptly vanish.

Crickets start screaming, all around. This island of dirt in the middle of the woods is almost the size of a basketball court. But logging didn't create this clearing. No, the trees just haven't dared to lay down any of their roots in this dirt. There are no stumps in this random circle of soil, and no other signs of vegetation either. No grass, no bushes, no weeds. Why not?

Bubba has never figured it out, but he knows this circle of soil well. He never *tries* to find it. In fact, he always tries to avoid it, but his select guests always seem to find it, on their own.

The Government claims it owns the Nowhere Woods, but no one does.

No one wants them. They never have. Something about this place repels most people.

Only the determined and the foolish seem to find their way here.

They step into the circle of soil. Dirt crunches under Bubba's boots. A big, dark boulder marks the other side of the clearing. It sits right on the edge of the tree line. But other than that big rock, and the dark brown, ashy dirt below, there's nothing in this circle. Nothing but them. The trees loom above them, like walls of a cage. The stars are piercing and bright. Bubba says.

"We should leave. Hogra likes to hunt at night, especially during this time of the year."

Then he finds the tree with an old man's face in the bark. It's the only way out of here. Three beards seem relieved by Bubba's exit ramp. They're tired after hauling all their bullshit through the woods. But Roy doesn't like this idea. Not one bit. He glares at Bubba, then yells.

"Fuck that. No one is going anywhere, until we kill Hogra the Terrible. Are we clear?"

The three beards nod, real slow. Then Bubba's ears perk up. The crickets shut up. The air is still. No one else has noticed the silence. Roy opens his mouth, but Bubba whispers first.

"Shh!"

And points ahead. Tall trees in front of them are rustling. At first, it looks like it's just the wind, but then a dark shape moves through the leaves. Bubba's neck tingles. He feels watched. The others see it too. Roy and Phil aim their rifles. Rex and Zeke point their cameras. They all get quiet. Even the wind

dies down. The silence is tense. Phil ruins it.

"Can you see it, Roy?"

"No. Can you?"

Bubba aims his deer rifle at the dark shape in the trees.

He isn't using a scope. He's had this same rifle for twenty years.

He knows it. He can work with the wind, point the little metal

notches on the barrel in *just* the right way. The hog is in his

sights. Bubba has it, but he waits, with his finger over the trigger.

He isn't startled when a hand taps his shoulder. Roy says.

"Not yet, Bubba. Do you guys have the shot?"

Bubba sighs. He warned the angry brick, but men like

Roy always break their promises. It's alright. Bubba was never

going to pull the trigger anyway.

"Not yet, sir. I need to change out the battery."

"Well hurry the fuck up and do it!"

Leaves rustle after Roy hisses. Idiots whisper. Bubba can

still see the dark shadow hiding in the rows of pale, glowing

spires. Goosebumps rise on his arm. It's still watching them, but this is something else. The air is getting electric. There's more than one observer out here.

Plastic snaps into metal. A low beeping noise follows a series of urgent whispers, then footsteps, closer and closer. Roy pushes Bubba's gun barrel down and says.

"Sorry, Bubba. But I paid to come out here, so I get the privilege of shooting first."

Bubba lets the darkness hide his grin. Then something snaps next to them.

He turns, but it's just birds, flying out of a tough little bush to their right. Roy, Phil, Rex and Zeke watch the birds as well. Bubba looks back to the hiding spot in the trees where he was aiming before, but the dark shape is gone. The others copy Bubba and turn. Roy yells.

"FUCK!!"

Bubba puts his gun down. He sniffs, and shudders. Sulphur. Rotten flesh. More sulphur. The foul, earthy aroma is heavy in the air now. It's almost time. Bubba pretends to get angry.

"Remember what I told you earlier, Roy?"

"I know, Bubba, but…"

"I TOLD YOU that if we had the shot, we had to take it, no matter what! And I *had* it, Roy, but you stopped me! You wanted the glory, all for yourself! Now you have nothing! It got away. Hell, if you had let me take the damn shot, you could've claimed the kill as your own!"

Roy tries to stifle his rage, but it doesn't work. Not this time. He screams.

"How *dare* you! I'm the one who's paying you, motherfucker! *I'm* the boss around here! And if we missed Hogra, it's *your* fault, Bubba! You're the guide, remember? And if you can't guide us to a clean goddamn shot, then what kind of a fucking guide are you?!?"

Roy waits for him to throw a punch, but Bubba just wants to laugh. Then his ears perk up. Leaves are rustling. Twigs snap, then the ground starts shaking. Shit. Something is coming.

It sounds like a galloping horse. But it's not coming from the trees in front of them.

No. It's behind them. Phil yells.

"SHIT!!!"

Bubba turns and raises his rifle. Trees are parting up ahead, like a flood is coming. But he sees the dark shape that's rushing at them. It isn't water. It was watching them earlier. It's fast.

Soon, it'll enter the circle of soil.

Phil fires. He never took his eyes away from his fancy, glowing scope. The gunshot cracks through the trees. A pained squeal echoes next. Phil's bullet hit the dark shape, but the galloping noise doesn't stop, or even break pace. It's only getting louder.

Branches snap, up ahead. Then, from a cloud of pale sawdust, a giant wall of flesh bursts into the circle of soil. The feral hog is charging at them like a battering ram. The basketball court feels real small now. Phil fires again. And again. The hog darts side to side. Plumes of dirt erupt all around it, not blood. Phil's first shot was lucky, but it wasn't enough. The hog is only twenty feet away from Bubba now. Those tusks look mean and sharp. He never stopped aiming his deer rifle. He has the shot. Bubba's finger is hovering over the trigger, but he won't pull it.

Then a second gun erupts in the circle of soil. It fires a long, steady stream of bullets. Roy screams.

"DIE, MOTHERFUCKER!!!"

He wasn't lying about his rifle being automatic, but Roy's aim is almost impressive. He's firing a lot of bullets, but none of them are landing anywhere near the charging hog. Stray, armor piercing rounds are just tearing up the pale trees that form a ring around the circle of soil instead. Bubba is shocked that Roy hasn't shot him yet, but that would be too easy.

The hog is only ten feet away now. Phil leans into his scope and fires again. This time, red mist erupts between the hog's cold, dark eyes. Its legs collapse out from under it. The hog hits the dirt and slides, towards Bubba. It's still moving fast. Will it crash into Bubba? No. That would also be too easy. Roy is still emptying his clip, and every one of his shots is still missing.

When the hog stops sliding, it's only two feet away from Bubba. Tops. It's laying on its side. Its hind legs are still kicking like a galloping horse. Bubba knows those swift, fierce kicks. It's the common, final act of a feral hog that got shot enough times to finally die. But they never really give up. They even make the grim reaper work for his paycheck. But soon, the hog's hind legs quit kicking. It goes still. Bubba leans over. He sees death in the hog's eyes, but he also sees sadness, and more humanity in its soul than in any of the men that he brought out here.

Bubba turns to them. Gun smoke is still drifting across their flashlight beams like fog. The four beards are stunned. Their mouths are hanging open. Everything around them is quiet, until Roy and his yes-men realize that the hog isn't getting back up. Roy shouts first.

"HAH! I got him! Hogra the Terrible is DOWN! I fucking got the son of a bitch!"

He hoists his rifle in the air, pumping it up and down with triumph. Phil clenches his fists. He looks at all his friends in the circle of soil. He knows that *he* had the kill shot, and he wants credit. But the other two yes-men already bought Roy's new fairy tale. Phil turns to Bubba next. He just smiles back. Bernie growls below. It's true. If Phil is smart, he'll let Roy take credit for this kill. Did anyone notice that Bubba never fired his rifle? Maybe. Maybe not. Roy yells.

"TELL ME YOU GOT THAT, ZEKE!!!"

Zeke goes pale. He looks at the camera's view-finder and rewinds the footage in terror, until he exhales like a man who dodged a bullet. Zeke gives a thumbs up and yells.

"YEP! You're gonna get a lot of likes on this one, boss! A lot of shares too!"

"Good. Now prop up this dead bastard and let's get some damn trophy shots!"

Roy claps his hands, and his yes-men scatter. He has no grace in victory. It makes the hollowness of his *triumph* even more comical. Zeke and Rex start propping up the dead hog.

"*Whoa*! Look! His fucking ball sack has *callouses*! Hogra was a *real* ladies man!"

They laugh as they work, but they aren't the only ones laughing in the circle of soil.

The dead hog has dark brown fur. It's big, maybe five hundred pounds. Zeke and Rex pry its jaws open, then wedge a rock between them. Now the hog's tusks and sharp teeth are frozen in a *snarling* pose. They prop up the head with sticks, then start placing lights. They've done this before. All over the world, to all kinds of exotic, endangered animals. It's why these clients are select. But they've never been to the Nowhere Woods. Or the circle of soil.

When the hog burst in here, he made a hole in the ring of trees surrounding this clearing. Bubba turns to it. Of course. The hole is gone.

Branches and pale spires healed on their own, when he wasn't looking. It's a miracle. It doesn't surprise Bubba, but no one else has noticed. Are the four beards starting to see other strange, disturbing things in the trees? Not yet. They're too busy with *Hogra's* body. As his yes-men prepare his trophy, Roy walks over to Bubba with his arms outstretched, and exclaims.

"You were right, Bubba! Hogra the Terrible is huge! Even bigger than you said he was!"

Roy is craving validation. He wants another toast to his great victory. Bubba replies.

"Oh, yeah. That's a big hog, alright. There's just one problem, Roy. It's not Hogra."

The circle of soil gets quiet. The crickets are still on mute. Roy's mood plummets from the heights of cloud-nine. Rex, Zeke and Phil turn to Bubba. The yes-men all have the same expression, a collective, wordless groan: *Why'd you have to go and do that, man?* Roy shouts.

"Bullshit, Bubba! You're just jealous, because *I* killed Hogra first!!"

Roy already believes his new lie. He could probably pass a lie detector test about it too. Phil is the only beard who looks afraid. He should be. Bubba points to the dead hog and says.

"Are you colorblind? Or do you just have goldfish memory? Hogra's fur is black and white. This is *brown*! Look at his hide, Roy! Look real close. Where's the Maine spot? Huh? Nice work, though. Real nice. You win. Go on now, sport. Go claim your prize."

"ENOUGH!! Shut your fucking mouth, Bubba!! Do you know who I…"

"Yes, Roy. I *do* know who you are. You're a poacher. One of the worst in the world."

Roy's eyes snap open, and darken. Now they look like twin gun barrels. He says.

"Watch it, Bubba."

"Oh I did, Roy. I saw all those animals that you killed. All the species that you personally drove to extinction, for money. For your ego. For likes and shares. I saw it all. But I just have one question. Where's your mask?"

Zeke and Rex raise their weapons. Phil darts his head around. He's looking for the exit, but only Bubba knows how to get out of the circle of soil. Roy smiles, and says.

"We add it in post, Bubba. So, you found my secret. What are you gonna do about it?"

Bubba shrugs when they aim at him, and says.

"I can't exactly go to the authorities, can I?"

"No, Bubba. You can't. I bought them *all* off, long ago. There isn't a single authority that matters, anywhere in the world, that I don't own. You can't touch me, Bubba. No one can."

Roy smirks. Bubba says nothing, he just listens to the sounds of the Nowhere Woods.

Branches snap in the distance, like bones. Nocturnal birds sing death metal songs to each other. At least, Bubba thinks they're birds. But whatever they are, he fears them a lot more

than the gun barrels that are pointing at him. Roy says.

"Are you done, Bubba?"

"I guess so, Roy. There's nothing else I can do to stop

you, is there?"

"Good. Because it's time for pictures."

Roy turns to the dead hog that his yes-men propped up.

Blood is pooling below the beast. Dark streams flow, from new

holes in its body. Rex and Zeke lower their guns. They start

setting up cameras and lights next to the dark boulder, at the

edge of the tree line. Phil exhales, like a real Switzerland. Bubba

listens. The air is still. Too quiet. Then he sniffs. Damn. It's

sulphur. He should get the fuck out of here. He stares at the tree

with bark like an old man's face. It marks the path that leads out

of the Nowhere Woods, and the truck. But Bernie growls below.

Not yet.

Sticks break close by. Shit. But it's footsteps, not a new

hog. Fuck. It's Phil.

"I believe you, Bubba. Is *he* still out there?"

He's whispering too close, but Bubba smiles at the terrified winner, and says.

"You'll see."

He gave these beards many exit ramps, but they ignored them all. Except Phil. He listens. He might survive. But maybe not. Maybe Phil is a secret asshole. Bubba will find out soon.

"What do you think of this shot, Roy?"

"Fuck that. My teeth look like shit. Next."

Roy, Rex and Zeke are hovering over the camera. But Bubba tunes out their vanity binge.

Phil is squinting. Oh yes. He finally sees something in the trees ahead. He mutters.

"What the hell…"

Then gasps. Phil is finally starting to notice what's been hidden in the pale trunks. Bubba doesn't need to look. He knows what Phil is seeing. Blood splattered on bark. Hanging entrails. Bodies on bodies, skinned, stacked and piled like trophies. Now that Phil looked away from his heat-sensing scope, he finally sees all the cold party decorations surrounding them. He stammers.

"Is…that…"

Bubba smiles, not at Phil, but at the dark boulder by the cameras and lights. Bubba says.

"Yes it is, Phil. Yes it is. I was wondering how long it would take you to notice."

Phil seizes up with terror. Roy and the yes-men around the camera keep yammering on.

"What about this…"

"My God! Who taught you to take pictures? A damn medieval peasant? Go back and…"

Cold air blasts across the circle of soil. A harsh, hurricane gust. It shoves Bubba back like an angry bouncer, and even makes Roy shut the fuck up. Pale spires are waving side to side, all around them. Leaves are rustling, but mostly falling. No one moves. That wasn't the wind.

Bubba hears someone gulp. Then the dark boulder starts moving.

It's growing. So is the stink of sulphur. Bubba knows what's coming. Regular feral hogs are masters of hiding, but Hogra the Terrible takes it to a whole other level. The giant, emerging beast *was* the dark boulder. When he's hiding, Hogra doesn't even breathe.

White spots emerge from the darkness. Bubba is just as scared as he was the first time. Phil turns around. He doesn't scream. He sucks in air like a dying vacuum cleaner, steps back and points at the moving boulder. Roy, Zeke and Rex turn to it next. The four beards were right next to their prize this whole time, but they only see Hogra now, when he *wants* them to see him.

Bubba tried to warn them. Now he stares at the undead monster with black and white fur.

Hogra the Terrible is longer than a tow truck, and taller too. He weighed over a thousand pounds when he died, but it's a lot more than that now. His head alone could crush the front of Bubba's truck. Hogra's tusks are diamond sharp traffic cones. His dinner plate eyes are glowing, like yellow fog lanterns. Their rage, intelligence, and hunger say it all. Hogra came back from *somewhere*. It changed him. Now he's far too clever.

His snout is puffing and dripping, but Hogra's nose doesn't just smell. It *sees* things in living beings, things that usually remain hidden.

His body is full of bullet holes. Dozens of them, maybe hundreds. But most of the holes are on Hogra's head. Bubba made four of them. Then he sees the famous dark spot on the beast's pale hide, shaped like the state of Maine. As if he needed any more confirmation.

Roy screams on a delay. Rex and Phil shriek next, but Zeke fires first.

The armor piercing bullet sparks when it hits Hogra. Something whistles past Bubba's ear, then the ground starts shaking again. That bullet just made Hogra angry. Now he's jumping and thrashing around like an angry bull. An earthquake starts every time his hooves hit the dirt.

Roy and Rex raise their weapons and back away from the bucking undead tow truck, but Zeke is frozen in place. He fires again. This time, sparks don't fly when the bullet lands.

Buzzing noises erupt instead. Hogra is many things, but he's also a mobile fortress. When he's hiding, they all shut up.

But not now. A cloud of locusts start pouring out of Hogra's mouth. Bubba feels a tremor, and sees the undead boar spear Zeke in the belly with one of his tusks. Hogra tilts his semi-truck engine head, and Zeke flies across the circle of soil like a bag of trash. He screams the whole way, until a loud *SPLAT* cuts him off. Bubba hears a slide, another crash, and rustling leaves. He doesn't want to think about the warm drops that hit the top of his head.

Lights are flashing where the *boulder* once sat. Now it's standing, and snorting.

One shot after another cracks through the empty night, and the endless pale spires. Fog drifts across shaky flashlight beams. It's not just from gun smoke anymore. Roy shouts.

"The eyes, Rex! Aim for the eyes!"

They're emptying their clips, but it won't be enough. Can bullets even put Hogra down? All the crusted holes in his body aren't a promising sign. And yet Roy and Rex are firing at will. Shots are landing all over Hogra's head, but they're only releasing plumes of sulphury dust, and opening up more holes for locusts to fly out of. Bubba waits for Hogra to go berserk, but instead, the massive beast stops thrashing around, and stands still. That's never a good sign.

Deep booms and flashing lights get replaced by empty clicking.

"SHIT!!!"

Rex and Roy fumble with their weapons, and Hogra the Terrible stares between them.

He's sizing them up. To those he deems *guilty,* Hogra has no mercy. He almost killed Bubba all those years ago. A deer didn't save him. Hogra almost tore through that helicopter and ripped Bubba apart. But then the hunting guide made a deal with the undead beast.

A deal that he's honored ever since. Bubba knew that Hogra was watching them when he entered the circle of soil. Now, he stares into the beast's yellow, dinner plate eyes.

Metal slides into one of the rifles. Something clicks. Rex starts firing again. He reloaded faster than Roy. Bad move. Hogra the Terrible turns to Rex. An ocean of fangs opens wide and chomps down. Rex's gun hits the dirt, along with his legs.

The rest of his body is in Hogra's mouth. Roy starts booking it, before the undead beast has time to chew. He screams.

"PLEASE! HEL...."

Bubba thinks about all the beautiful beings that Roy gunned down, and smiles.

Another earthquake begins. Despite his size, Hogra the Terrible is swift.

In two strides and less than a second, he catches up to Roy. Bubba sees a glimpse of pure terror in the poacher's eyes, before Hogra bites him in half. Blood sprays all over. Everything turns crimson. Bubba cringes from the taste of copper. Then Hogra the Terrible starts running.

Bubba can feel it. The tremors are impossible. He can barely stand, but he opens his eyes through the dark muck. Hogra is stampeding around the circle of soil. The beast is fast as hell, running in a tight loop, and kicking up a lot of dust. Soon, Bubba can't see anything at all. A dense wall of dirt has blanketed the clearing, like a brown blizzard. He shuts his eyes and waits.

It doesn't take long.

When the tremors die down, something small thuds on Bubba's work boots. He feels it twitching. He opens his eyes and looks. It's a hand. Roy's hand, twitching in a final act of bodily defiance, like the other hog's kicking hindlegs. Then Bubba sees it, wrapped around one of those bloody fingers. A tan ring, made from a rhino's horn. Roy's prized ring. Now it became someone else's trophy, but fingers and hindlegs don't matter now. A cold gust makes Bubba look up.

Hogra the Terrible is standing three feet away from him. Phil is shaking next to Bubba. He's covered in blood too. Hogra caught Roy three feet away from them. Maybe less. The poacher's body parts are even closer. And now the undead beast is breathing fast, judging them.

Roy's mangled head and upper torso is dripping and falling from the side of Hogra's mouth, like drool. Locusts are still flying out of that ocean of fangs as well, along with all the crusted bullet holes littered across his body. Others are joining their torrential flow. Moths and wasps. Flies and waterbugs. Their collective buzz is nauseating. It's even worse, because most of the noise is muffled. It's coming from inside of Hogra. The best is yet to come.

A dark spot is growing between Phil's legs. He pissed his pants. Bubba probably pissed himself too, but he has other things to worry about right now.

Hogra's yellow eyes are probing him. So is that oozing, puckering snout. Roy, Rex and Zeke are dead. Is that enough? Or will the big, undead feral beast finish the job and kill Bubba and Phil next? Hogra the Terrible snorts. A cold blast of sulphury air says he's thinking about it.

Bubba has been here before, awaiting his judgement in this same circle of soil, but that doesn't make it any easier. No, he gets more terrified every time that he's here. Bubba knows that he's pulling his string of luck back even tighter. Eventually, it'll snap.

Is this the day? Maybe. Only Hogra the Terrible knows the answer.

Bubba stands still and awaits his verdict. But he doesn't want to look into those yellow lanterns, so he stares down. A beam of light is shining between Hogra's legs. A severed hand is still holding onto a flashlight. Bubba looks where it's pointing. He blinks. Holy shit.

Bubba sees the remains of Roy, Zeke and Rex. Their body parts are scattered all over the circle of soil. So is their blood. Bubba shivers. Not from the gore, or the brutality itself. No, it's the way these bodies are *presented*. It doesn't look like they got butchered and scattered in a sudden ambush. Their body parts and blood are forming the rough outline of a shape.

It's a spiral.

The pattern is right there, in the circle of soil. Hogra the Terrible is huge, but somehow, he made all the blood splatters and body parts land in the shape of a spiral. He's methodical, like a cat. Hogra propped up Roy and his yes-men, like trophies. Just like they did to the brown hog. Roy was convinced it was Hogra. He believed his own lies, until they caught up with him.

Bubba looks where the cameras were set up, and blinks. Holy shit. The hog that they shot earlier is gone. Somehow, when Hogra kicked up all that dust, he also made that body disappear.

A blast of cold, foul air almost knocks Bubba over.

Hogra just snorted. He takes a heavy step, and walks even closer to them. This is where it could all go wrong.

Then Bubba hears a strange chortle. He looks down. Something small, grey and black is standing between him and Hogra the Terrible. It's Bernie. The giant boar's glowing yellow eyes look down. Hogra stares at the odd, stinky cat.

Bubba feels nervous and protective over his little friend, but he knows better.

This is how it has to be. Bernie and Hogra the Terrible have a strange relationship.

Instead, Bubba turns to Phil and says.

"Roy said that you never went out hunting with him and his men before. Is that true?"

Phil is covered in blood, but his exposed flesh is white as a ghost. He's in a place that's far beyond terror, but somehow, confusion helps Phil find the strength to croak out.

"Yep."

Is he realizing what Bubba and Bernie have been up to the whole time? Bubba shrugs.

"Well, we're about to find out if you're telling the truth."

Hogra snorts and gets closer to Phil. Bernie stares up at him too. This is Phil's moment of judgement. Is he guilty? Bubba is leaning towards innocence, but his voice isn't what matters.

It all comes down to Hogra the Terrible. What will he say?

Bernie chortles below, and rubs his dirty, matted coat of fur against Phil's leg. Bubba watches his reaction close. Most assholes cringe when Bernie gets close to them. Not Phil. He bends down and pets the strange cat's head. Hogra the Terrible snorts like he made a decision.

The beast turns away. Bubba feels the ground shake before Hogra starts running.

He charges past the bloody trophies that he shaped into a spiral, and crashes into a group of trees. Hogra uproots them all, and keeps running, deeper into the Nowhere Woods. The dirt is still shaking from Hogra the Terrible's stride, but the tremors get softer and softer. Eventually, they fade to nothing. Bubba blinks. Bernie is rubbing against his leg and purring, loud as hell.

Bernie only purrs like this when he sees his big friend.

After a couple more seconds of silence, the crickets start chirping again.

Bubba and Phil turn to each other. They start running without saying a word.

Bubba heads for the bark that looks like an old man's head, and Phil follows. They leave the circle of soil and vanish into the strange, densely clustered pale trees. Branches snap and pop. Leaves crunch below. Bubba tries to think about nothing, but before they left, he looked at the group of trees that Hogra smashed. Those pale spires were healing themselves already. He keeps running. Time passes in a sealed vacuum, fast and slow at the same time. Trees blur together. Branches stab his arms, and ribs. Crickets are screaming all around. Their message is clear.

"GET THE FUCK OUTTA HERE!"

Bubba's legs move on autopilot. He doesn't know where he's going, but somewhere deep down, he does. By the time he shoves through the last cluster of pale branches, he's delirious, and standing at the edge of madness. But at least he made it out of the Nowhere Woods.

Bubba cries when he sees the ridge again. His truck is right up ahead. Then he gets dizzy, and tired. *Very* tired, like jet-lag. They weren't flying, but they went somewhere else. It took a lot longer to get to the circle of soil than it took to leave. Did the trees seduce them, take what they wanted, and chuck them out? Bubba doesn't mind. He'll take this ridge, and the stream below.

The stars above are dim. They've been smothered by something strange. Clouds.

Bubba smells a sweet, alien scent in his nostrils. Moisture. Is it about to rain?

He opens his truck door. Bernie hops in first. Bubba goes next, closes the door, shuts his eyes and exhales slow, with as much gratitude as possible. He makes absurd promises about his future behavior. The truck's other door opens. Phil gets in and screams immediately.

"WHAT THE FUCK JUST HAPPENED?!?!"

Bubba laughs with a laconic drawl, then replies.

"I know, right?"

Hogra the Terrible has only spared one other man, besides Bubba. Why Phil?

The horizon ahead flashes bright blue. Thunder rumbles, in the next breath. Then drops start landing all over Bubba's truck. They're falling faster and faster. Holy shit. It's raining.

It's been months since this land saw its last storm. Bubba smiles and watches. Phil is waiting to hear more about the madness that they just escaped. But when he realizes that more isn't coming, he looks ahead too. Then, with a sudden, jerky move, Phil pulls down the sun visor above his seat. It's dark out, but it's as if Phil was drawn to the sun visor, and its secrets.

Glossy photos spill down and land all over his lap. Photos of Roy, posing with dead leopards, rhinos, giraffes, and many other beautiful beasts, who died for no reason. Some show Roy masked, as the world saw him, but most don't. Someone leaked the unedited images of this poacher, and sent them to Bubba. Now Phil is looking at the photos of Roy. His eyes bulge, then he turns to Bubba, real slow. Phil says.

"What the…"

"Oh yeah! Thanks for reminding me about those."

Bubba snatches the glossy pictures from his passenger's lap, then reaches below his own seat. Bubba pulls out an old book. It's a thick photo album with a worn spine and a black cover.

It's branded with a simple, crimson shape. A spiral.

Bernie sits in Bubba's lap. He opens the old photo album, and starts turning pages. It's filled with photos of men who are also posing with dead, exotic animals. Bubba flips through his past accomplishments and hunts for the first blank page, where he can add his latest trophies. Bernie watches him flip through the old photo album. The strange cat is purring, loud as hell.

Bubba scratches Bernie's dirty head. The stinky cat's enthusiasm makes sense. They did it all together. Phil looks terrified, but also curious. He asks.

"Who are those guys?"

"Poachers and assholes, just like your old boss."

Phil's eyebrows raise. He's starting to put it all together. He says.

"Wait. You mean, you *knew* what was…"

"What was going to happen out there? Oh yeah. Bernie and I planned on it."

Phil looks between Bubba and Bernie with building alarm in his eyes. He stammers.

"So, you..."

"Oh yes, Phil. It's a hobby, of sorts."

"Why?"

"Why not, Phil? Fuck those guys. Are you grieving about them?"

"No, but..."

"Roy said it himself. He put his life into his own hands when he came out here to hunt the legendary Hogra the Terrible. He failed, and paid the price. It's the way she goes, isn't it?"

Phil nods. He was horrified by this idea at first, but it's starting to grow on him. He pets Bernie on the head. The strange cat smiles at Phil, in Bernie's own, bizarre way. Phil says.

"So, Hogra the Terrible really *is* a zombie feral hog, isn't he? How did he come back?"

Bubba shrugs and speaks the truth.

"I don't know, Phil."

"What do you mean you don't know? I thought..."

"You thought wrong. I have no idea. It's not my place to know, and Hogra the Terrible isn't much of a talker. You wanna go back into the Nowhere Woods and ask him yourself?"

Phil shivers at the thought, then he looks down and Bernie and says.

"Is your cat..."

"A zombie like Hogra? I don't know. Maybe. I found him like this."

Bubba thinks about the spot on that eerie, empty east coast highway that compelled him to pull over all those years ago. That pile of sticks. He keeps talking.

"Someone abandoned Bernie, but I rescued him. Is he a little bit stranger than most cats? Sure, but no cat is normal. Bernie is Bernie. I love him, and he loves me. Dead or undead, it makes no difference to me."

Bernie is staring at Phil like a guy who wants a fight. The cat lets out a long, drawn out *YOWL* of a meow. Bubba doesn't speak cat fluently, but Bernie's message is pretty damn clear.

"BACK OFF, SHIT-HEEL. IT'S NONE OF YOUR

FUCKING BUSINESS."

Phil got it too. He nods like he's trying to appease a mad dictator, then keeps stammering.

"But won't they find out? Won't they come looking for you? For us?"

Bubba smiles.

"Who? How will they know where to look? Don't you remember, Phil? Your people booked this trip in cash, and used fake names. Did they tell anyone where they were going?"

Phil frowns in deep concentration, then a knowing realization relaxes him. He says.

"No. Roy made us all sign forms that said we'd keep quiet about this adventure. No contact with friends, or family, and no social media posts either. Our accounts were locked. He even confiscated our phones, and gave us burners instead, with restricted internet access."

"Well, there you fucking go! We have a system, Bernie and I. And it works. All the lovely critters in the woods are busy taking care of their bodies, and then…"

Bubba points at the rain drops hitting the roof of his truck, then says.

"We'll get cleaned up back at the airfield. It's all side roads from here. No cops."

Bubba almost forgot about the blood all over his clothes. He always does.

He's used to it, by now.

His clothes always turn dark brown and crimson red when he comes back from a trip into the woods with Bernie. Thunder rumbles in the distance. The road ahead is empty and desolate, and the truck's tank is half full. Phil nods with a blooming, crooked smile, then says.

"So this is what you do? You find the most heinous, vile and cruel poachers you can dig up, and lure them out here to these woods, so Hogra the Terrible can kill them?"

Bubba shrugs.

"You got it, Phil. That's our racket. Sure, someone might come along and ask questions about Roy. It's happened a couple times, but when I start explaining my business to curious local officials, and try to sell them on the myth of the giant, undead feral hog that I take people out to hunt? They always get squeamish, and can't find the exits fast enough. They don't wanna end up in the tabloids. And when it comes down to it, they don't really give a fuck about dead poachers either. Who does? Do you? Like I said, Phil. Bernie and I have a system. In fact, we only have one loose end left from this trip. You. Will you keep your mouth shut?"

Phil opens the truck's window, throws his red hat out into the rainy badlands, then says.

"Well, Bubba. That all depends. Are y'all hiring?"

THE SNOW GLOBE BLOCK

Dylan is behind. She double-parks her delivery van and looks around the quiet, suburban block. It's more green than grey. She sees tall trees and *homes*. Driveways and lawns. She hears children playing. Is she still in America? This neighborhood is like a village in a snow globe. An artificial creation, frozen in time. Pleasing to look at, and completely isolated from the city around it. Until people like Dylan come along, to deliver their packages. Must be nice.

There's even a vintage muscle car, parked up the block. A red Chevy, from the seventies. Dylan smiles. It's her dream car. *One day*. Then she checks her phone. Shit. This is the place.

A green moat of manicured grass surrounds this pastel blue mansion. It's shaped like a castle. It has a ridiculous porch, and more windows than Dylan's whole apartment building. The backyard must be spacious, quiet. Do crickets drown out the sirens back there? Or the bombs?

If she finishes this drop fast, and hustles to the next block, she *might* meet today's quota. The packages never stop piling up. It's merciless, like draining a tub with an eyedropper. But then she remembers the wooden crate. This is her last drop. Her shift is ending soon.

When Dylan is wearing this purple, hi-vis vest, she's neutral. She can cross barbed-wire checkpoints, all over the city. Every warring faction wants the goods that Baikal delivers. But once her shift is over, her company uniform vanishes, on its own. So does her free pass, and a woman who looks like Dylan can't get stuck in McKhaki territory. Yet she stops, and looks up.

A kite is flying. It reminds her of a simpler time, before Civil War Two.

The floating triangle has familiar colors, and shapes. It's the American flag.

These days, it's a rare sight. Dylan can't remember the *specific* incident that made this country finally break apart, but no one was surprised. States and cities shattered. A patchwork clusterfuck of warring factions emerged. Rivers of blood have been flowing ever since.

Civil War Two has been raging for years. No one is winning. They're too busy fighting. Everyone, that is, except for

Edgar Alice, Baikal's CEO. Guns, bullets, food, water, toilet paper. Baikal delivers it all, to the combatants. It's the only neutral party in this conflict. It has to be.

How else will all the rival militias get the supplies they need, to keep the war going?

Dylan frowns. She hates it here. She wasn't happy in the Before Times either, but she should've had more fun, before it all went to hell. She feels a rattle, in her chest. Is it an 808?

Shit. Someone just pulled up next to her delivery van. It's a camouflaged Hummer.

Sirens are mounted on its roof, along with a big, fifty-caliber machine gun. Dylan waves, at the *neighborhood patrol*. Men with helmets, armor, and digital visors don't wave back.

They're scanning her. *Assessing her threat level*. Do they think she's a mercenary, like them? Tires screech. The Hummer takes off down the calm, green block. They found another *disturbance*. Kids laugh, nearby. Do people live in this snow globe block to isolate themselves, from a crumbling world? Of course. That's *always* been why people move to the suburbs.

Dylan frowns, at the pastel blue castle. Can she go through with this drop? Who lives in that place? What did they do to afford it? She looks down. There's faded text, on the sleeve of her shirt. *Dylan's Famous Biscuits*! It's the last surviving artifact, of her family business. She had a bakery, once. With regulars. Even a secret menu. People loved it, but Baikal destroyed her store, just like every other small shop in America. Dylan should quit. Their abuse is relentless. They make her do evil things, like this *delivery*. But she stays, and follows Baikal's orders, to protect her sons. Without her, the war will swallow them.

Dylan gets out of her van, and opens the back. She finds the package that's destined for this pastel blue castle. Unlike all the other boxes in here, it isn't cardboard. It's an old, wooden crate. It made a long journey, and passed through many overworked, desperate hands to get here. Dylan has seen this type of oak case before. She always gets them, on these *special* drops.

She knows what's in there. *Don't think about it. Just take it to the finish line*. The case is heavy, but she starts hauling it across the green moat. Sprinklers hiss, on both sides of a stone path. Birds sing, from branches, until the ground shakes. There's a deep, menacing rumble, with crackling aftershocks. But it wasn't thunder. No one in the city can *really* escape from the war.

There's movement, in the corner of her eye. Blindfolds rattle, in a neighbor's window. Someone is watching Dylan, and her truck. It's engine is still running. The back is open. They want what it has, and they can't be the only ones. Metal clanks, behind her. It's a rolling, ticking noise. Dylan doesn't need to turn to know. The delivery van is printing a metallic, armored shell. An *anti-theft protection device*, that she can't control. She's locked out. All alone out here now.

Dylan stops at the castle's front door. She braces the oak crate with her knee, to reach for the doorbell. But when her finger gets close to the button, she hears voices, in the house.

"...And that's exactly why the task force got shut down, Bob!"

"Dammit, Al! Listen to me. We were *this* close to..."

"What? Catching the power brokers? The big shots? *HA*! We never closed a *single* case!"

"Now, wait a damn minute…"

"Numbers don't lie, Bob! And we didn't have any! Just costs. A *whole* lot of those!"

Dylan should drop this box on their porch, ring the bell, and leave. Baikal is watching, and their punishments are creative. But she knows what'll happen when she hits the *delivered* button on her phone, and Dylan can't do it. Not yet. She's nosier than most, and can't stop now.

These guys are nuts. A police task force, that only went after rich people?

In the Before Times, the idea would've seemed noble, but insane. But now?

"That's it, Al? You think we should've gone after shoplifters instead? Jaywalkers? It…"

"I wanted our task force to *succeed*, Bob! But you didn't listen to me, or anyone else! You wanted to catch the big fish, or nothing. And that's what we got. Shut down, shit-canned, and buried, right before the war started. *Thanks for your service!*"

Al laughs, with venom. Dylan sighs. Her finger is hovering over the doorbell. What is she doing? She needs to go. That Hummer will be back soon. What's she waiting to hear? A secret, that could end Baikal? *Please.* These oligarchs probably just offended Edgar Alice at a party. Even if their task force was real, it would've been doomed. Maybe, one day, someone will turn their idea into a TV show. Popcorn propaganda, to make regular people think that justice exists.

"But we *almost* got the big one! We were..."

"*Almost* doesn't get you shit in this city, Bob! *You* taught me that! And yes, our task force definitely got shut down, because suits upstairs were protecting Baikal. But *you* gave them..."

"*FINE*, Al! It's *all* my fault! Happy now? No? Then why didn't *you* take the promotion?"

The belligerent voice quiets down, on the other side of the door. Bob fills the new void.

"I know why. You want to be liked. You don't have the guts to make hard decisions. We all knew that Edgar Alice was the puppet master, and I didn't want to waste time."

Dylan takes her finger away from the doorbell. *Now* she knows why she's here. She was ready to finish this job, and move on. But now? She isn't sure. The locals won't be busy forever. The clock is ticking. Dylan has to make a choice. She looks up. The kite is gone. Did it drift away? Probably. It's like her. She's *usually* a delivery driver, but sometimes, Dylan has to kill people. Always with exploding wooden cases, like the one in her hands.

"Why am I here, Bob? Is it some *smoking gun*, that'll blow this whole thing *wide open*?"

"It is."

"So what? Even *if* you have some real evidence, what good will it do? The institution that we worked for is *long* gone. Who will listen to us now? Some local fucking warlords?"

Birds call, from a nearby tree. Al's optimism knows no bounds, but Bob replies.

"*Exactly*! I want to get them all together, in one neutral space, to talk. I want to…"

"You're gonna invite them *here*?"

"If that's what it takes, so be it."

Whoa. Dylan waits for more, but the men get quiet. Are they checking to see if anyone's listening? They aren't doing a very good job. She's standing by their front door, and isn't hiding.

"Well go on, Bob! Let's hear what you've got!"

"Baikal isn't just profiting from Civil War Two. They started it, and have been *managing* it, this whole time. Edgar Alice bombs, starves, and divides the American people, with targeted, data-driven precision, to make this war eternal. His mercenaries assassinate any local leaders who unite their people, or try to make peace with rival cartels. It's his *whole* business model."

"No shit, Bob. I'm *shocked.* But, where's the proof?"

"It's all in that banker's box. After the leader of the Sunshine Estates was killed, and her peace plan collapsed, a whistleblower came forward. They gave me documents, videos, and receipts. They died to reveal the truth about Baikal. We need to gather every warlord, show them all this shit, and ask simple questions. Why are we killing each other? Why fight over scraps, and blocks, when we could fight Baikal? Together, we can crush them, and end this damn war!"

Dylan blinks. Damn. It's a good idea. Jeff, her *community leader*, would love to meet Bob. Birds shut up, in the trees. The kids stopped playing. The snow globe block just went quiet.

Why? This wooden crate is heavy. Dylan shifts her stance. *CREAK*!

Shit. She hears footsteps. The door flies open, before she can run. A big man is glaring at Dylan. He has short red hair, and a bushy moustache. Blue jeans, white shirt. Thick neck. Big arms. He seems familiar, or maybe he's just typical. He looks down, and draws a pistol. Shit. Does he know about Baikal's *special* oak boxes? He aims at Dylan. Fuck. She yells.

"Wait a minute! Just wait!"

"Drop the box! NOW!"

"That's a *bad* idea. Please! I can…"

"What the fuck is going on, Al?!"

A man with grey hair runs up to the door. He's skinny. Tweed suit, frantic energy. Yet his eyes seem thoughtful, even idealistic. But when their gaze meets Dylan, it's icy, dead serious. This must be Bob. A hammer clicks, as Al yells.

"What do you think? Look down! Remember *those* crates? She was sent here to kill us!"

Guess this is it. Al is right, and Bob looks like a good detective. He'll know if Dylan is lying. She can't even go out in a final blaze of glory. She can't reach her phone without dropping the box, and the bomb won't go off, until she presses the *delivered* button. Dylan doesn't even want to blow them up. She wants to help them, but how can she say that, without it sounding like a desperate lie? Tires screech, in the distance. Bob claps.

"Wait a minute…No way! It's *her*!"

"What the fuck are you talking about?"

"Don't you see it, Al? Look at her shirt! It's right there, on her sleeve!"

Al leans forward, and squints. His gun is still aimed at Dylan, but his eyes pop. He yells.

"Holy shit! *NO WAY*! You're the lady who made those biscuits!"

Al lowers his pistol, after thinking about food. Dylan sighs. She should've known that it would happen like this. Her chest is thudding. It must be her heart. What would these guys have done, if they didn't *know* her? But they do, and they love her all over again. Bob keeps talking.

"I *told you*, fuck-head! You remember the one with that..."

BOOM!

Someone tackles Dylan. *BOOM*! As she falls sideways, hot, sticky liquid splashes across her face. *BOOM*! *BOOM*! *BOOM*! Thunder is punching her chest. It's deafening, relentless. She lands on the porch, but the oak crate breaks her fall. A body crashes on top of Dylan. It's Al.

Glass shatters above. Splinters fly. He just saved her. From what? She looks past him.

Bob is flailing. He's getting ripped apart. Dylan turns away. A barrel is flashing, on top of a Hummer. It's the same militia thugs that scanned her earlier. Al rolls over, hides behind a splintering column, and aims his pistol at the blasting cannon.

Sawdust sprays his face, but he's still darting his head around, looking for an opening. A decent target.

A shell whistles past Dylan's head. She looks down, and grabs the wooden crate. Fuck it. She gets up, heaves, and throws the box at the Hummer. It lands on the sirens, then tumbles through an open sunroof. She ducks, and hits the red, *package delivered* button on her phone.

Everything gets bright, and hot. Burning wind shoots past. Glass shatters. Metal clanks, up and down the block. Boiling kettles are shrieking in her head, but Dylan opens her eyes.

A black cloud is rising, in the middle of the street. Ash is raining down, like dark snow.

The Hummer is charred, and smoking. It was a direct hit.

The war finally came to this pristine snow globe block.

Silence reigns, for now. Dylan blinks. Her face is wet. So are her clothes. Shit. It's blood. Bob's remains are splattered all over his porch. Al turns to her, proud and furious. Dylan speaks.

"I can help you organize a meeting with the warlords. Fuck Edgar Alice, and Baikal."

Dylan doesn't know where those words came from, but she spoke them with conviction.

"Can you *actually* make that happen? Tonight?"

"My block's warlord is nuts, but Jeff hates Baikal. She'll *make* the others listen."

Al grins like a maniac, and bolts through the pastel blue castle's shredded door.

Dylan peeks inside. It was nice, once. A beam falls, into a plume of dust. What did Bob do, to afford this place? Will Al tell her? Maybe he won't. She shakes her head, and gets up. Tea kettles cool down upstairs, but now she hears a high-pitched, demonic buzz. It's distant, for now. How many drones are coming? Dylan feels a breeze, and looks down. Shit. Her uniform is gone. Her shift ended. Are her kids playing right now? She hopes they're having fun.

Up ahead, in the blackened street circle, Dylan spots her delivery van. The blast also shattered its armored shell. The *lock* around the company vehicle is gone, and the engine's still running. The back is open. Those boxes are full of canned food, water, toilet paper, ammo, and porn. Curtains part, in nearby windows. Dirty fingers poke through sewer grates, in the road. Sirens are coming too. Many genres of looters will soon swarm on her van, and over its spoils.

Dylan always wanted to quit Baikal. Now she has to. Al emerges, with an overflowing banker's box. It has papers, hard drives, plugs. Will she be able to keep her promise? He says.

"C'mon! We gotta go!"

They start running. Now that Dylan sees Al in a rush, she knows who he is. He *was* a regular in her shop. A bad one. A real source of dread for Dylan, before real problems consumed them both. He *definitely* remembers their petty rivalry, but a common enemy has united them. Maybe others will follow. Al holds up the keys like a remote, and hits a button. Headlights flash, ahead. It's a red Chevy. That old muscle car, from the seventies. Dylan grins.

STAFF ONLY

A creaking noise startles Ron. Footsteps? He looks around the small, dark movie theater.

It's still empty. There's no one in here. No one but him and his wife, Lorna.

And yet, he's cramped. Ron is a big guy, and this seat is tiny. Its hard plastic armrests are jabbing into his sides, penning him in. What are they watching? This theater feels like a crushed soda can. Its dimensions are all wrong. The dark walls are loaded with Rorschach shapes. The ceiling is puffy. It looks like it's made of cotton candy that was painted black.

"Do you smell it *now*?"

That was Lorna. She's whispering. *Here she goes again.* Ron sniffs, to appease his wife, but this time, something awful creeps up into his nostrils. It has notes of rotten meat, aged for weeks in a hot dumpster. He'll be damned. Lorna was right. She's been complaining about a *smell* in here, ever since the movie started.

Lorna sees his revulsion. Triumph gives her a twisted sort of smile. She yells.

"I *told* you!"

Then covers her mouth. Ron doesn't fall for her timid gesture. Lorna is waiting. She wants him to say it, out loud. *You were right.* But Ron just shrugs. What's she trying to prove? It's probably just bad, old plumbing. Shit pipes, showing their age. His belly growls.

Oh yeah. Where the hell is his food?

The waitress vanished. She appeared when the movie started, like an apparition, took their order, then left through a door. A door to Ron's right. It's been taunting him ever since.

STAFF ONLY.

How long ago was that? It feels like *hours*, but Ron can't tell. His phone is dead. This movie just keeps going, on and on. It's ancient, and painful. Why did he pick it? What happened, before he walked in here? Fish pop into his head. His gut howls. It's fed up too. Ron says.

"Where the hell is our…"

"*SHH*!!"

Lorna shushed him like a stern, feared librarian. *Uh-uh.* Not today. Ron yells.

"WHY!? We're the *only* fucking people in here!!!"

He gestures around the dark, empty theater. That felt good. He's been whispering, ever since this goddamned movie started. Not anymore. Ron knows what he has to do. He says.

"I'm gonna go find out what happened to our food."

He gets up, and squeezes down the narrow aisle. Lorna whispers, and tugs at Ron. All he sees is *STAFF ONLY.* It's a challenge to his manhood. Fuck that. He's going in there, to find that waitress. The food doesn't even matter. This is about *respect.* She forgot about him. She's hiding in there, and getting high. Ron knows it. He can't wait to torment her. It's how he gets pleasure. He hates his life, so he lashes out. Usually at Lorna, but more often, it's *the help.*

Ron shoves the big door. It barely budges. Damn. *STAFF ONLY* is heavy as shit. A beam of light cuts into the dark theater. He hears odd, creaking noises. From the room beyond? Fuck it.

He takes five steps back, then charges, like a battering ram. His shoulder erupts in pain, but the door only opens halfway. Lorna chuckles behind him, but whatever. It's enough.

Ron slides through the *STAFF ONLY* door.

The next room is bright. He blinks. It has matte-black walls. The floor is greyer than a concrete parking garage. This room is small, but it has three options. It's a junction, of sorts.

Ron sees two staircases ahead. On the right, narrow steps go up, to a dead-end wall. Why build a stairway to nothing? Is this a funhouse? The left steps go down. It's a short trip. The area below is dark, except for a red *EXIT* sign. Its glow catches on something metallic. Is it a door?

Ron smacks his head. This isn't some evil shadow realm. It's a movie theater. This is the *service section*. The world of the help. Isn't it? Where's that damn waitress? Maybe he should've checked the lobby first. Shit. *THE LOBBY*. When he was out there buying tickets earlier, he saw a fountain. It wasn't the kind with pissing cherubs. No, it was *classy*. It had spitting fishes.

Ron looked into their pool, to see how many coins were sacrificed to them over the years, but he didn't see any change. It was just rocks. Dozens of stones. Maybe hundreds. They all had colors, and circles. Rings of green, blue, and brown, with black spheres in the middle.

The white ovals were eyes. The fountain was full of them.

Ron turned away from their collective glare. He didn't look back, or tell Lorna. Now he's here. Something is wrong. He can feel it. Between the dead-end stairs, and the matte-black walls, this place is weird. Vague dreads swirl in his mind. Is he just being paranoid? He *is* trespassing, after all. He doesn't belong here. He fears no authority, but he does fear something. What?

It's down there. Beyond the door, highlighted by the red *EXIT* sign. It's calling Ron.

He turns right. He's next to a long, narrow closet. The smell that Lorna kept going on about hits him, all at once. It's an altar of gore in there. A metal table, writhing with scavengers of the dead. Ron gags, but he can't look away. He was just sitting on the other side of this wall.

Lorna's still in there. What were they watching? All he remembers is a headache, and restless limbs. Was it a horror movie? A comedy? A tragedy? Do they still make those? Ron doesn't give a shit, he just pays for movies to keep his wife quiet. What now? He yells.

"HELL-*OOO*?!?!?"

His voice echoes, then fades. No one replies. Not even Lorna, and she's *right there*. Did she hear Ron? Did anyone? What the hell is going on? Does *anyone* work here? Did they all go out for a smoke break, and never come back? This place felt like purgatory, until he found this collection of flies and entrails. Ron turns back to the bright junction.

"*HEY*!!! What the fuck are you doing back here?!?"

He grabs at his heart. There's a man at the top of the stairs. Ron runs. He jumps down six steps, shoves a metal door, and bolts down a long, empty grey tunnel. The lights are harsh. He sees stone steps at the end of the hall, and speeds up. He *has* to get there. It's more than survival.

"You *really* don't want to go back there, man!"

Ron stops in his tracks. Where do those steps go? Why was he running? He turns around, to face the voice. Some stoned idiot is standing in the doorway. Long, messy hair. *Professional* sweatpants, and paint-splattered kitchen shoes. The stoner turns away, while muttering.

"...Maze of fucking ghosts in there..."

THUD!

Fuck. That was the door. It just slammed shut. Ron runs back, and tries to rip it open, but the handle won't budge. There's paint on the metal. Thickly coated crimson, with claw marks.

The lights flicker slowly. After every flash, the darkness appears to be moving. He yells.

"Hey! Let me out of here! *I'll sue*, you fucking burnout! You, *and* this whole company!"

Something is breathing, behind Ron. Shit. He spins around. It's the stoner. What the fuck? Now the idiot is wearing a top-hat, and a shiny suit. Like a cheap Vaudeville performer, from a hundred years ago. How did he get there? Who slammed the door? Ron gulps. The eyes under that top-hat have a pull. It's like staring into twin black holes. The Vaudeville Stoner smiles, with an empty mouth. He removes the hat, and reaches for something inside.

Fuck. Ron turns right. There's a pink door next to him. It has a sign. *STAFF ONLY*.

Ron shoves it open, and bolts into darkness. It's loud. The door closes behind him.

Lorna darts her head up. What was that? She thought she heard a scream. It didn't come from the movie. She looks around the dark theater, and notices how alone she is. Its seats are arranged in a strange shape. Four long rows are pressed close together, right up against the big screen. She's in the last row, but she's been craning her neck up the whole time.

Every seat in here is the worst one in the house. Who designed this place?

All the dimensions are wrong. It was built to punish the viewer.

The movie isn't helping. It's notorious for being comically horrible, but it's just horrible. Where the hell is Ron? He flipped out, fifteen minutes after the movie started. Why?

What's he doing now? Lorna hasn't heard shit, except for that noise, that could've been a scream. Was it?

Is Ron lost? Maybe food isn't why he's looking for the waitress. *Bastard.*

Lorna snorts with contempt, and gags. The smell came back.

It's acrid, piercing, with notes of wet garbage, and burning rubber. The kind of stink that lingers. What is it? She feels prickles on her neck. None of this seems right, but what can she do?

Plenty. Lorna gets up. She's going to find her fucking husband.

"The Master won't be happy…"

The voice startles her. It came from the screen. A scruffy man is chuckling up there. He has a soggy brown hat, a misshapen jacket, and potato sack pants. He's hobbling towards her, with luggage. Awful jazz fills the theater. It gets louder. The saxophones warp, and slow down.

They sound deep now, monstrous. The strange man slides to the left, along with a car, some mountains, and the sky.

They all drift across the glowing wall, until the screen goes white.

The movie vanished. Why not?

Lorna turns away from it, and follows a shrinking cone of light.

There's a small window by the ceiling. Is anyone up in the projection booth? *CREAK*!

She hears footsteps, somewhere in the theater. Fuck this. Lorna bolts down the narrow aisle, and shoves *STAFF ONLY*. It hurts, but the door opens, enough for her to squeeze through.

She blinks. It's bright in here. The air is stale, charged with static. A voice cries out.

"NO! *PLEASE*!!!"

Shit. That was Ron. Lorna's eyes adjust. She sees stairs. That's it. This room is cramped, but tall. The door clicks, behind her.

"STOP!!!"

It's like she stepped through a cubbyhole that leads to an attic. Red brick walls surround this eggshell staircase. The steps are made of warped, bubbly linoleum. Where do they go?

Lorna looks up. There's a dark, square portal, twenty steps above her.

"LET ME…*ARGHHHHHHHH*!!!!!"

Screams echo, but where's Ron? It sounds like he's getting skewered.

Apparently, he made a new friend. Someone just like him.

Lorna should climb these steps, or go back into the theater, but she listens, and smiles. She remembers Ron's *accidents*, with ironing boards, and frozen bottles. The unrelenting abuse of waiters, crossing guards, postal workers, dog walkers. The relief when it wasn't her, followed by the guilt of not stopping him. If he got his *kicks* out on the help, his later eruptions, at her, were mellow. Sometimes. It's shameful. She wishes that it wasn't true, but it is.

Oh well. What could make him scream like that? It could come for her next. Fuck.

Lorna turns around, and pulls at the door. *STAFF ONLY* doesn't budge. Is it stuck?

"NOT *THAT*!!! *ANYTHING* BUT…"

It sounds like her husband is screaming, right behind these bricks. Lorna starts climbing. Linoleum steps sink and hiss below. People who work here use them often. Her mind goes back to waiting tables at that casino. To those twisted, hazardous passages, designed for *the help*.

Lorna keeps climbing. *CRUNCH*. What now? She looks down. *Oh*. Someone spilled their bucket of popcorn. She follows the kernel's path. *CRUNCH. CRUNCH*.

When the stairs end, Lorna stops, at the mouth of the portal. *Yes*.

There's a long hallway up ahead. She sees pink, tiger striped walls. The floor is a black runway, stretching out for a block. It's the lobby. A hall with many doors. Each one leads to a different theater. It's where she came from. The last place she saw, before this nightmare began.

Then Lorna sees the glass doors, at the end of the runway. The exit. *BOOM*!

Walls rattle, all around. That noise was deep, and muffled. Was it a fighter jet? Did something blow up in an action movie? Are actual bombs falling, in the streets outside?

Maybe it's a fire. That'd be nice.

She should run, but there's a big poster to her right.

She's never heard of this movie. It's a visceral image, a bloody scene of sex, death, and sin. Its horrors would take weeks of study to fully digest, but maybe it isn't a poster at all. It's more like a painting. The kind that belongs on a mantle, in a strange sort of church. One with stone, candles, straw, and blood. Not much else.

It's hard to miss, but Lorna didn't see it on her way into the theater. Did she walk past it? Shit. Maybe it *wasn't* there, before. She doesn't remember seeing pink, tiger striped walls out here either. Is this building constantly changing shape, when its visitors aren't looking?

CRUNCH!

Lorna gulps. Her feet didn't make that sound. She hears wet, smacking lips. She turns.

There's a tall man standing right next to her.

She backs up, but the tall man keeps chewing. He's blocking an arched doorway. How long has he been there? Who is he? He's still too close. He has long, greasy hair, and a soggy brown hat. Loose grey coat, potato sack pants. He's grinning, but there aren't any teeth.

Lorna blinks. This tall man looks familiar. How? He stinks like a tomb. His long, bony fingers are holding a metal bowl. They feed a dark flake into his mouth. *CRUNCH*!

How is he making that sound, without any teeth? She peeks into his bowl.

It's full of black, shriveled kernels. The smell comes roaring back. Lorna tastes tires.

Her head throbs, and her vision spins. It was burnt popcorn. A stink that never leaves.

"You shouldn't be here."

The voice is hollow: the sound of wood in a tall church. Lorna looks up, and into his eyes. Her spine turns into a glacier. Fuck. They're vacuums. Whirlpools. She stammers.

"I…I know. I'm sorry, I'm just…looking for my husband…"

The chewing stops. Quiet spreads. It's electric, tense, waiting for more. That Dust Bowl outfit doesn't match his splattered kitchen shoes. A dark, gooey shape falls on them, like bird shit. Is it chewed-up popcorn, from his gut? If she shoves

him, will her hand go right through?

Oh. Lorna saw this hillbilly in that shitty movie. It's *the*

Master's creepy servant. What was his name? *Gordo*? He was

holding luggage, before the screen turned white. Did he

somehow jump through the fourth wall, into reality? Who is he?

What is he? Shit. Who is his *Master*?

Something starts beeping. It's loud, relentless. A timer.

She hears bubbling pots, and sizzling meat. Old instincts kick in.

Is someone gonna get that?

"I know where Ron is hiding, Lorna. He isn't far."

Terror floods her spine. Gordo knows their names. How?

Smoke is pouring, behind the tall man. Is it a kitchen? What's

burning back there? Does she even want to know?

"What's wrong? You should be honored! This joint ain't

cheap! Ron must've done something *real* nasty to get these

tickets, to someone with *important* friends on our side!"

Laughter echoes down the lobby. What *side* is Gordo

talking about? How *did* Ron get these tickets? Lorna can't

remember. Her mind is a drugged carnival. Her ears start ringing.

It's Gordo's stare. Twin black holes are reeling her in, like a fish.

The tall man smiles. That slimy, toothless mouth, and those dark, whirlpool eyes make the rest of his face look like a mask. Maybe it is. Is there something even worse, hiding below?

Gordo takes off his soggy brown fedora, and reaches inside, like it's a magician's top-hat. His arm tenses up, as he grabs hold of something. It's long, hairy, carved, and gashed.

She sees an anchor tattoo on a pale wrist. Fuck. It's Ron's arm.

Lorna starts running down the lobby.

It's empty. Doors pass, on the left and the right. They're all shut. It reminds her of a school hallway. More twisted paintings blur by, but she keeps charging towards the exit.

"Don't leave now, Lorna! The big show is starting! You DO NOT wanna miss *THIS*!!!"

Gordo's voice echoes. Lorna gulps, but keeps running ahead. What *show*?

THUD!

Doors fly open, all around her. Up and down the lobby. Lights flash, in the theaters beyond. Did every movie in here just end, at the same time? Is this Gordo's *show*? No.

Goosebumps rise, as Lorna runs. Crowds are stampeding out of every theater. But it isn't people. White rocks are flooding the lobby. Dozens, maybe hundreds of them. They're floating. Like eggs, drifting in outer space. Lorna is surrounded. They all have colors, and rings. Brown, blue, or green, with black dots in the middle. It's a pattern. They're hovering in pairs. Every duo has a matching color. It's eyes.

Their collective glare is magnetic.

Lorna hears whispers behind whispers, and knows what they are. She feels it. In the back of her neck, and in her soul. What are the floating stones talking about? The films they just saw? The timer keeps beeping in the kitchen, as Lorna sprints through the eyes. She can't avoid them all. She tastes sulphur. Rocks touch her flesh. They feel like glass. They're cold. Colder than ice cubes. Colder than a blast of angry, polar air. They move like a school of fish chasing her.

Lights flicker, above. The walls are swirling. Neon pink tiger stripes warp into exposed steel beams. Then bricks. Lorna keeps charging. She's halfway to the end of the lobby.

A cacophony of whispers are right behind her. She won't look back.

Their language is unknowable, but the tone is clear. Curious before; now angry.

But Lorna sees those glass doors, up ahead. Her salvation. Her exit. Fuck. Prison bars came down, over this theater's gates. They're sealed shut. She's locked inside of this place.

What now? An angry swarm is rushing behind her. A floating parade of hate. She speeds up. She's heading right for a crash, but fuck it. Why not? Hitting a solid wall sounds *a lot* better, than letting them catch her. The gate is close. Here it comes.

Lorna shuts her eyes. She braces for hard pain, and a head-on collision, but runs through something wet. Like a cloud, or a waterfall. Her feet hit a surface that feels familiar.

Is it a *sidewalk*? No. It can't be. Lorna stops running, and opens her eyes.

It can. She's out in the street, right in front of the movie theater. What the fuck?

Thunder rumbles, in the distance. She looks side to side. She's standing under a big marquee. Waterfalls are flowing, from every direction. It's pouring out here, and now she's joined a small, ragged crowd of bums taking shelter in this awning.

The breeze is crisp, but Lorna remains dazed, until cold water splashes her. She blinks.

White orbs speed past, six feet away. Another typhoon washes over her. If Lorna didn't stop, she would've booked it, all the way into oncoming traffic. But, how did she get out here?

She turns. The metal shutters are gone. Green boards are blocking the theater's gilded entrance instead. They're covered with posters and graffiti. It's a plywood sculpture, crafted by years of neglect. Walls like this usually grow around construction sites, like weeds. What the hell? None of this makes sense. What did she run through? Prison bars, a wet membrane...

She walks up to the boards, and touches them. Will they ripple, like water? They sag, under her finger. The plywood is soft, with a filmy sludge. There's a window to her left. A diamond-shaped portal. Unlike the rest of the wall, it's clear. An island of mutual respect. A necessary window, to appease the people's curiosity. It's a bad idea, but Lorna peeks.

She sees a dump. An empty wasteland. It's full of dust, splintered debris, and empty beer bottles. But its shape is unmistakable. There's a fountain, topped with spitting fish.

People whisper, behind her. Lorna turns. She sees glassy eyes, animated by fear. The bums hold their liquor bottles close, like protective relics. They're staring at her, like she's a collective hallucination: a ghost. *Is* she? Lorna asks.

"What year is it?"

No one answers. She turns back to the plexiglass diamond.

"Why are you looking in there, lady? That place has been abandoned for a *while*!"

Lorna doesn't reply. She's playing with a ring, on her left hand. It's tight, uncomfortable. When did she get it? She hears the name *RON*, like an intrusive thought. Who's that? What happened in there? Vague terrors flicker and vanish in her mind, like Polaroids in a bonfire.

What was she running from? What did she escape? It's all fuzzy, with the urgency of a complex dream, fading fast. Maybe something won't *let* her remember.

That building might *look* abandoned, but somehow, to Lorna, it feels *alive*.

Maybe everyone forgets what happens in there, if they're lucky enough to leave.

She turns around, and gasps. The crowd grew, under the marquee's waterfalls. By *a lot*. When she got out here, *maybe* six people were gathered by this shelter. Now, it's dozens. Some are wearing dirty rags. Others have suits, and mini-skirts, but their eyes all look the same. It's a lost, empty gaze. Everyone in this crowd is wasted, yet focused. They're all staring at Lorna.

The crowd is too dense to run through. She's surrounded. Trapped by the front of a stage, in a sold-out show. All the suits, rags, and skirts are swaying to the same rhythm.

They almost topple over, but never *quite* get there. It's hypnotic. Why are they all so interested in Lorna?

She steps back. Dozens of glowing screens emerge, from purses and pockets.

They're all showing a scruffy man, with a brown hat. A legion of fingers hit *play*, as one.

"You can never leave…"

Alone, that haggard voice wouldn't rise above the storm. But together, as one, his voice is amplified. Booming up and down rainy streets, like a sheriff or a tyrant.

Lorna's heard that line before. Where? Does it matter? She keeps backing up, until her shoulders touch the soggy, plywood wall. Synchronized footfalls come next. The liquor puppets are marching. Their glare is a whirlpool. A black hole. Lorna turns around, and looks up.

Exposed bricks are peeking out, above the green boards that she's pinned against. It's the building's original exterior. Lorna squints. There's something up there. It's hiding in a dark gap, between two bricks. It's a rock. A white oval, with a black ring. *Oh.* If she runs into the theater's ruins, she can get away from these liquor puppets. Lorna starts climbing over the green

fence.

TRASH PANDA

Noah ducks out of the kitchen. Fryers pop and sizzle behind them. Small printers keep shrieking. Cooks in white aprons scream about buns. There's an ugly side door ahead. It says *emergency exit only*, and this isn't a drill. Noah shoves it open, and steps outside.

They wince. It's sunny. The breeze is gentle, crisp. It doesn't even smell like butter. Noah looks down the tree-lined block. Old brownstones are casting long, angular shadows. Birds chirp, all around. It's glorious. Too glorious. Noah has to focus. Their break is only five minutes long.

They walk on auto-pilot, towards the park. They can't light their joint *this* close to work, but there's a cracked stone wall at the end of the street, and a familiar bench. It's Noah's spot. They always smoke there. Usually, half a joint is enough. Not today. Their job is reliably awful, but this shift has been special. Their whole section is probably still snapping and waving. Every ticket they sent to the kitchen started two fights, at least. And so far, the best tip they got was a buck. Noah looks down. Oh yeah. At some point, they also burned their hand. The wound is red, angry, exposed. The restaurant's first aid kit was empty. Is Mercury in the microwave again?

Noah clenches their fists. This hangover isn't helping. Why the hell did they drink that damn Soviet spray paint last night? What was that guy in the Hawaiian shirt talking about again? Whatever. Noah needs to smoke, and be alone. Now. They look ahead, and see their bench. Shit. They also see a crowd. Yuppies, skaters, and homeless people have formed a circle around the bench. Only half of them have their phones out. They're focused. On what? Is it a musician? No, their fascination is too profound. A crowd this random usually grows around a fight.

Noah walks faster. They're excited, until they get close to the bench. It isn't a brawl.

Everyone is pointing at the ground. At something moving. Noah squints. They see dark fur, and a bushy, striped tail. Whoa. It's a raccoon. A big one. Usually, these are wily

critters. Fast ninjas, with posable thumbs. Not this one. It's

staggering on the sidewalk, like a lost drunk.

"Is that racoon rabid?"

"Maybe it's mating season?"

Noah leans on the cracked stone wall, lights their joint,

and inhales. The crowd goes on.

"Should we call the police?"

"Animal control?

"What's their number?"

"Look it up!"

Noah exhales, and coughs. It burns, but it also feels like

they just dropped a pair of fifty pound dumbbells. As the layer of

piss and vinegar that saturated the world gets washed away, a

cloud of smoke washes over the crowd. Some wrinkle their

noses. Others smile. Will anyone give Noah a fake, passive-

aggressive cough? They wait, but the crowd is glued to the show.

The raccoon steps from bricks to dirt, then stumbles into

a tree. It startles her, after a two second delay. She tries to climb

the tree, but only succeeds in hugging its trunk. Some laugh.

"Shut up, *asshole*! This isn't funny!"

"Call someone!"

"Who?"

"What's their number?"

Every yuppy, skater, and homeless person has their own idea about how to *handle* this, but no one will act. They just want to watch, and pretend to help. Noah inhales again.

They've never been this close to a trash panda. Usually, raccoons move like bandits. Not this one. She wobbles back onto the sidewalk, and keeps stumbling in circles. A slow, rambling dance. It seems like she's given up. She's been dulled, and ground down, by the relentless forces of life. Noah is pinched by a sudden wave of sadness. Is it pity for this animal, or themselves?

They hear movement, and look up. The crowd is shuffling, around the bench. Everyone is turning side to side, and blinking. As if they all just woke up in a strange place, at the same time.

Noah burps, and tastes the party last night. They gag, but then remember. That guy in the Hawaiian shirt gave them a psychology lesson. He pulled Noah aside, and offered them a drink. His booze smelled like spray paint. Writing on the label looked Soviet. Noah took a sip, and regretted it right away. The Soviet spray paint tasted like death. The guy started quoting Sartre, but he smelled like a shart. Shartre pointed at a nearby group of punks, and said.

"Watch. In a couple minutes, they'll all go quiet, and have no idea why!"

Shartre sipped his Soviet spray paint, and rambled about strange forces in human brains. About breaks, needed to process new information. Noah stuck around to watch. It only took a minute for the guy's prediction to come true. All the punks went quiet. They looked confused.

Shartre had a haunted chuckle. He said that learning too much about psychology had driven him insane. Whatever. Noah shakes their head, and looks around. The sidewalk is empty.

They're all alone out here. What happened? Everyone cleared out, except for Noah, and the trash panda. It looks like Shartre was right. After ten minutes, everyone stopped talking, and wondered what the fuck they were doing. They all left, while

Noah was doing the same thing. What now? There's still a burning ember on the tip of their joint. Fuck it. They look down, at the forgotten attraction. The raccoon darts her little head, side to side. Is the critter wondering where her audience went? Is she sad that they left?

The raccoon straightens her posture. Dark, beady little eyes sharpen.

She turns to Noah, and winks. What the fuck? The raccoon leaps. She lands on the same tree that she tried to climb earlier. Now her claws dig into that bark, like an expert. She scales the trunk, jumps over Noah's head, and plummets into some bushes, on the other side of the stone barricade. Leaves rustle. The furry bandit vanishes into the big park beyond. Noah blinks.

Rusty gears turn, upstairs. Pieces click together. *Whoa.* That raccoon just pulled a prank on Noah, and the whole crowd. Why did she pretend to be sick? Just to fuck with them?

Shit. Noah shakes their head. Their five minutes ran out a *while* ago. They can feel it. They sigh, and start walking back to work. *Oh yeah.* They drop their roach on the sidewalk, stomp it out, and pass by a tubby old man, with flushed cheeks. He stops, and yells.

"*HEY*! Scumbag! You gonna fucking pick that up?!?"

Noah wants to punch this geezer, but they learned from the raccoon. They run up to the wrinkly drunk bastard instead, grab him, shake him by his shoulders, and shout.

"*HELP ME*! A goddamned *raccoon* just bit me! I think it had *RABIES*!"

The old drunk shrieks, squirms away, and takes off running down the block. Noah smiles. Maybe they should act like a trash panda more often. The rest of their shift is going to be fun.

THE MECHANICAL AMERICAN

Credits roll on Earl's favorite show. He chuckles in his recliner. That last gag got him good. He turns to see if his family is laughing too, but there's no one else in his living room.

It's full of paintings, lamps, leather-bound tomes, and other artifacts, but clutter can't mask the emptiness in here. It wasn't always like this.

A deep boom erupts outside. *CRACK CRACK CRACK.* Earl tenses up, but the gun shots end, fast as they came. Echoes fade. It was a short skirmish. Voices are yelling in the street now. Sirens start screaming next, but they aren't outside.

"COMING UP TONIGHT ON AMERICA'S FAVORITE SHOW, WE HAVE…"

Earl mashes buttons on the remote. In a perfect world, the TV would shut off, but he lives in this one, so it just gets muted. A big silver badge is flashing on his wall.

PIGS is starting up.

Earl looks down. He stares at the purple carpet below his slippers. Anything to avoid that iron badge, get it out of his mind. *PIGS* makes him remember why this house is so lonely.

He almost gets angry, but sighs in his recliner instead. Earl feels like that sad old bear, on every box of *Sleepy Time* tea. His ears start ringing. The sirens are getting louder. What the fuck? He checks the wall screen, but it's still muted. What's making this noise? Has Earl finally lost it? Then the fogs lifts upstairs. He recognizes the sound. Damn. It's his doorbell.

Someone is hitting that button like it gives out free money.

It's the middle of the night. Who the fuck is out there?

Earl starts rising from his comfy chair. It's a process. The plush recliner doesn't want to let go of him. He moves slow, and groans loud. He almost shouts for someone to *get the damn door*, a phantom reflex. Nobody is here with him now, except for the Mechanical American.

He isn't much of a replacement for family, but Earl would never say that out loud.

He gets out of the chair, and avoids the Mechanical American's eyes. They're hollowed-out caverns, but it doesn't mean that they're empty. Far from it. There's more going on in those caves than any other pair of eyes that Earl has ever encountered. They're terrifying.

And the rest of his roommate is worse.

The statue arrived on his porch one day, in a big wooden crate. It was taller than Earl. Wider too, and long as a grand piano. A pacing delivery driver gave him a paper to sign. He asked who the box was from, but she shrugged. She said: "*check the return address*," and fled.

The slip was blank. He shoved the big crate into his living room, and pried it open with a crowbar. The Mechanical American was waiting inside. There was a note as well. It was short.

Earl shivers, and keeps moving. His front door is close. He dodges piles of laundry and junk mail, scattered across the floor, like landmines. He's been alone in this house too long. He looks above his windows. Lights are glowing, in every metal box that he installed. That's good. Earl worked in home security systems, before he retired. It's a thriving industry. A lot of high-tech toys fell out of his company truck, and he used them all in his home. It has many surprises, for unwanted guests. He almost smirks in the hallway, until he passes D'Angelo's portrait.

Fuck. Earl can't look at his son right now. The doorbell is still shrieking. He yells back.

"I'm coming, you crazy bastards! Hold your damn horses!"

The door starts thudding. It's rattling on its hinges. Earl narrows his eyes. Is this the day? Debt sharks and Witnesses don't knock like this. Men with badges, flashlights, and guns do.

Ten years ago, Earl's life changed forever. *PIGS* shot his son, thirty nine times. One bullet for every US state and territory. And *the most popular show in America* played it all.

People talked about D'Angelo for weeks. They gossiped about *stats*, and various *points* that murderers earn. But a wrinkled lady in a grocery store said something that really stuck out.

"*That thug should've complied!*"

Earl buried his anger then, and hasn't let it out since. He told himself that he was saving it all up, for something big. He even built that secret sub-basement, and made dramatic plans. But he never acted on them. Dee died a long time ago, and now Earl just sits in his chair, every day.

Even if he gets a chance to burn it all down tonight, would he? He stops at his front door.

"OPEN UP!"

Earl slides the *who the hell is this* chain into its latch, and cracks it open.

Everything turns white. A shiny boot wedges itself into the small opening.

"WAKE UP, FUCKHEAD! We're here about a shooting. Let us in, *NOW!*"

A tall man is barking. Half of his face is a dark visor. This cop flunked charm school faster than most. From the iron cross neck tattoo, to the black riot armor, he's a typical specimen. Shoulder pads, gauntlets, and an expensive helmet. His Kevlar vest is topped with a silver badge.

There's a pistol in his holster. Its barrel is still smoking. Earl thought he recognized those bullets, earlier. This big cop fired the rounds, that are now magically justifying his presence. It's the circle of life. But he isn't holding a flashlight. The blazing, painful glare is *behind* him.

Earl winces, from a sharp, metallic stink. It's burning circuits. *Oh.* It's a spotlight. He hears low voices, in his yard. There's a film crew out there. Wow. They work for *PIGS*.

Burning circuits bring back decades. Earl worked for a magician, and studied that trickster. His timing. His tone. Every tool he used to capture, and twist a crowd's attention.

Earl shouldn't let these cops into his house. But if he tells them to *fuck off*, they'll probably kill him. It's *technically* illegal, but laws don't apply to law enforcement. And if these guys look weak in front of the cameras, ratings will plunge. Their audience loves blood. They crave it. But they haven't killed Earl yet, and he hasn't budged. They must need an excuse.

"Out of the way, Grady! You're fucking up the shot!"

Someone is yelling from the yard. *Grady*? The big cop scowls, turns around, and shouts.

"Excuse me!?!"

"You heard me, asshole! *I'm* the guy who makes you look good, remember?"

"Listen up, you…"

The barbarians keep shouting, but Earl's ears start ringing, even louder than them. Why? According to his mother, it means that someone is thinking about him.

He turns to his living room, and the hideous chess master. Shit. She was right.

The Mechanical American is staring at Earl. Those caverns are dark, and deep. The statue is tall, even though he's sitting behind a desk. There's a nest of gears, wheels, and wires in that oak cabinet, but he doesn't use them. He must've looked a lot different, before the fire. Half of his face is crisp, and sagging. The rest is worse. He used to wear a turban, but it melted over his scalp. Now he has a blue Yankees cap instead. Someone put it there, but it wasn't Earl.

Was it the Mechanical American? His arms are waiting, on both sides of a chessboard. Onyx pawns and ivory rooks are in formation. Can anyone tell that those bishops and knights are made of glass? Chemicals give them color. The white pieces live by the Mechanical American. He always goes first. He won't have it any other way. Do any of these barbarians play chess? Earl turns to the tall mass of riot armor that's blocking his door. Grady never stopped shouting.

"…And let us do our goddamned job, or I'll blind you all!! What'll it be?"

Earl hears shuffling in his yard, but no one speaks. Grady scoffs.

"That's what I thought."

The big cop isn't looking at Earl. Grady doesn't fear him, or the cameras. But Earl is old enough to remember a time when cops were afraid. Back then, if they got filmed killing people, it caused outrage. Sometimes. Some of them got fired. Some even got jail time. Some. But that was before Americans became numb to pixelated snuff films. Soon that numbness turned into pleasure, cravings, monetization, and profits. *PIGS* was born. It didn't take long to become the most popular show in America. And they want Earl to be their next, short-lived guest star.

"*PIGS* WILL BE RIGHT BACK, AFTER A WORD FROM OUR SPONSORS!"

A voice called out from the living room. Modern TVs won't let him mute the ads.

"THE NEW, PEARL HARBOR PICK-UP TRUCK IS..."

The big cop still has his back turned to the door, but it's time. Earl speaks.

"How can I help you, *Officer*?"

A frowning mouth, with a square jaw, turns back to Earl. Grady barks.

"It's simple, *old man*. LET US IN, *NOW*!"

The big cop snarls. Grady doesn't know shit about Earl, but it's clear what character he *expects*. They want a senile old shut-in? *Game on*. Earl looks behind the big cop, and exclaims.

"Wait, AM I ON *TV*?!?"

He's a bad actor, but it's an easy sell. The excitement is real, he just wants them to think it's because he wants to be famous. Just like everybody else. Grady sighs, like his conspirators. These thugs must encounter camera-thirsty victims often. They just never make the final cut.

"BITE DOWN ON OUR NEW, DELICIOUS CRUNCH MELT SUPREME!"

It's foolish to think that an appearance on *PIGS* will turn one into a star, but it fits.

When it airs, everyone has to watch it. No one can change the channel. No wonder it's the most popular show in the country. But how many people actually like *PIGS*? How many would stand up to protect it? Or them? Grady says.

"Don't worry about the camera, Mister…"

"*Don't worry about the camera*? Are you kidding me!? I'M ON *TV*!!! *HI DEE*!!!"

They don't even know Earl's name. Was it pure chance that brought them to his door? Who cares? They're here now, so he waves. He's truly excited. Grady asks.

"Who the hell is *Dee*? Your wife?"

"No, *officer*. D'Angelo is my son."

Earl takes a long, deep breath. Grady smiles, wide enough to reveal yellow, pointed teeth.

"Oh, really? *How sweet*, and sad. Do you think your son wants to see you like *this*?"

Something snaps, deep inside of Earl. Does Grady know what he just stirred up?

"Like what, *Officer*?"

"Really? Do we have to spell it out for you?"

Acting is getting easier. Earl is fully immersed the role of the befuddled senior. He asks.

"Spell *what*? Who are you people? Did I win a contest? Is this some kind of a quiz show? What the hell is going on here?"

Grady smacks his head.

"We're *police* officers! And we're here to ask you some fucking questions!"

"Why didn't you say so?! Come on in!"

Earl slides the chain, opens his door, and steps back. He waves them in, slow and steady, hands visible. Agitated men with riot armor and a sweaty film crew barge into his house. Nostrils flare, as soon as the barbarians get through the door. Their contempt is loud.

They're disgusted. The smell in here is repelling them. Good. The sage must be working. Earl walks down his hall. A mob stomps behind him. They think he's crazy, but harmless. The door clicks, behind the last cop. Earl peeks over his shoulder. A red circle blinks, above the latch. Motion sensors hum. Silent protocols are being engaged, all over his home. Now, that door will open up one more time, before things get interesting. He hears voices, ahead.

"WHO WILL BE PUNISHED ON TONIGHT'S SPECIAL, *LIVE* EPISODE OF *PIGS*?"

They're going live? That's new. The wall is silent, when Earl enters his cluttered living room. Soon, it's swimming with rude, stomping life. They snicker at his tomes, and artifacts. Will they actually look inside the books? He does a head count. He sees three cops, two camera operators, a guy with a spotlight, and a lady holding a long pole, topped with a fuzzy square.

Grady is the largest among the seven of them. He grins.

"I wouldn't be *too* excited about the camera, if I was you."

The big cop's eyes are hidden behind his dark, shiny visor, but Earl sees enough. All that hate and cheap training is just there to obscure a scared bully, who never grew up. Earl says.

"Excited? About what? Before you start telling me about my feelings, have a seat. Relax, before you…uh, what is this again? Therapy? Legal advice? Are you here about *the rapture?*"

The seven barbarians fidget. Another visor with a mouth whispers to Grady. He says.

"I think we have the wrong house."

They all start stomping down the hall, towards the front door. No one notices D'Angelo's picture. Earl *should* just let them go, but then a spotlight shines on the Mechanical American.

"Whoa! What the fuck is *that?*"

Everyone stops, and turns. The camera man zooms, and focuses. He's a pro. He knows good TV when he sees it. The sound lady holds her boom mic over the hideous, melted statue.

She presses her headphones closer to her ears, and narrows her eyes. Earl exclaims.

"*That*, my friends, is the Mechanical American! He's the rarest artifact in the world!"

The barbarians look impressed, except for one camera operator. Her jaw is clenched. Her forehead is dripping. She's scared shitless. Two of three cops seem excited, except Grady.

"*Check*!"

They all jump back. The sound lady throws off her headphones, but she can't look away. No one else can either. The Mechanical American just talked. Gears start clanking, like an old grandfather clock. The robed statue is moving. A melted head turns, side to side.

Someone yelps. Everyone else is sucking in air through their teeth.

The Mechanical American's right hand rises, then falls. *THUD*! The collision echoes across the living room. *THUD*! *THUD*! The statue is pounding on his table. He's impatient. He wants to play chess, but can't, until a challenger sits on that chair, across from his desk.

THUD! Earl looks between the seven barbarians. One armored man is reaching for his holster. The other goes for the shotgun on his back, but Grady is smirking. Why? He shouts.

"Calm down, everyone! I know about this thing. It *is* a rare artifact, but this old fool has it all backwards. It isn't called *the Mechanical American*, it's the Mechanical Turk!"

Earl is surprised. Has Grady actually read a book? Now the others look confused.

"The Mechanical Turk?"

"What the hell is *that*?"

Grady opens his mouth to reply, but Earl cuts him off.

"He *was* called the Mechanical Turk, but it's a long story, and you guys must be tired! Have a seat. *Please*! All this standing around is making me nervous..."

Barbarians murmur. Earl looks down his hallway. D'Angelo is still smiling in that frame.

Earl saw him in the morgue. His son's body was laid out on a shiny slab, with thirty nine bullet holes. For no reason, except ratings. Earl's hands should be shaking, but they're steady.

"*Unit oh-two, come in!*"

Grady frowns. The static voice came from a walkie-talkie, strapped to his Kevlar vest. The big cop holds the radio close to his mouth, and says.

"Unit oh-two here, what the fuck do you want?"

Static voices reply with coded gibberish. Earl doesn't know what it means, but the seven barbarians look excited. Did they just learn which unit got chosen for tonight's live episode? The collisions stop. The statue paused his tantrum. Why? Grady says.

"Sure, old man. We could all use a break. *Right*, boys?"

The crew keeps standing, but the cops sit down quick. Earl's furniture is dusty, but comfy as hell. Grady plops into the big recliner. Is it because he can tell that it's *Earl's* chair? Probably.

Earl walks over to the statue. He picks up a small, coffin-like box from the oak desk, then turns around. All seven barbarians are staring at the Mechanical American. They're transfixed.

"What *happened* to it?"

"Must've been a fire. A big one."

Is it his melted face? Or those deep, hollowed-out caverns? The crew recoils, but keeps their gear focused. Is every screen in America about to play their footage? Earl sees red dots above both lenses, glowing just like the metal boxes, hanging over every window. Earl says.

"Don't worry, folks! He just wants to play a game of chess. Who's up first?"

No one volunteers. Earl smiles. Even now, centuries later, the Mechanical American can still command a crowd's fear. The old bastard has still got it. Does Earl? He hopes so. He looks at the small box. Legends say that it powers the statue, but Earl knows the power of misdirection.

"Quit being coy, Grady! Tell us more about this *Mechanical American!*"

"Dammit, Riggs! It's called the Mechanical *Turk*! Hundreds of years ago, people thought that this thing was a robot. A robot who could think, and beat anyone at chess. The Turk was famous as hell. Everyone wanted to play it. It beat Napoleon, *and* George Washington!"

Grady looks smug. He loves the sound of his own voice, so Earl cuts in.

"It was actually Ben Franklin."

"Whatever. For decades, people were convinced that the Turk was an unbeatable chess master robot. That is, until Edgar Allen Poe investigated it, and exposed the hoax."

"What hoax, Grady?"

"What do you think?! A person was in the machine! Broke chess masters got paid to hide out in there, and control it. After the secret was revealed, no one cared. Now the Turk lives on, in the squalor of fine homes such as this one, fed by sad geezers who desperately need company."

The barbarians chuckle. Grady adds.

"Sorry, old man. Did I spoil the magic for you? Did I scramble your *lecture*?"

Earl shrugs. Only one being in this living room is offended right now. He says.

"No, because you're wrong. That hoax wasn't the *real* Mechanical American. This is."

The time is now. Earl holds up the small, coffin-like box, for all to see. Grady screams.

"Hands where I can see them!"

The big cop tries to bolt out of the recliner, but flails instead. It won't let go of Grady. Earl keeps his hands still. Before the other two can get up, to reach for their guns, he exclaims.

"Sorry, guys! I didn't know that an old man could scare you so much!"

It's almost funny. The cop are the only people in here with armor, and weapons. And yet, they're more afraid than the film crew. When shame makes them relax, a little, Earl goes on.

"This box controls the *real* Mechanical American. He's been hidden, for hundreds of years. Wolfgang von Kempelen invented him, and Wolf stared into this very same box, when that machine played. They said it had supernatural powers. An old lady even fled a match, because an *evil spirit* possessed the chess master, from this box. But despite, or perhaps *because* of those fears, the Mechanical American became famous, fast. *Everyone* wanted to play him."

Earl opens up the small coffin, and peers inside. He smiles, then goes on.

"But fame changed Wolf. He started acting strange, reclusive, as if his own machine frightened him. He tried to hide the Mechanical American, by pretending that the statue needed repairs, but the demand was too great. So, Wolf told everyone that he *dismantled* it."

Earl shuts the box, and keeps talking.

"The truth is that he tried to burn it, but it didn't work. Not completely. When Wolf *had* to make the Mechanical American return, he didn't fix the original. He made a second machine. *That* one toured the globe, with a new host, and was eventually exposed by Poe. But the original was buried, and forgotten, until now. This is it. And unlike that clone, he isn't a hoax."

The living room gets quiet. Earl isn't acting anymore. Are the seven barbarians realizing that their first impressions of him might've been wrong? Grady speaks, from the recliner.

"So you say, old man. Well, I…"

"You can call me a liar Grady, but the hack who got exposed by Poe never used *this* box, during his act. He said that he didn't need it. But maybe, just maybe, he was afraid of it too."

Wind blows, outside. Nervous bodies shuffle in the living room, until Grady says.

"So, how the hell did *you* get it? Why do you call it the Mechanical American?"

Earl thinks about the note that he found, in the massive crate that appeared on his porch. It was short, simple, typed, and signed with three letters. *TMA.* He says all that can be said.

"Because this is where he wants to be, and that's what he wants to be called."

"*Oh*, I get it! This is the part where you try and *scare us*, right?"

Grady spoke like he's confident, unafraid. He's doing a lot of acting now. Earl looks down, just to make sure. He's standing on a square white carpet, with a smeared brown stain. It doesn't look like chocolate. Few in their right mind would stand here, except Earl. He laughs.

"Am I really *that* threatening? I guess so…"

Tension grows in the living room. Are the cameras still rolling? Hopefully. Earl goes on.

"…But I'll give you guys a chance to prove that you aren't afraid of this *hoax*. I'll let one of you challenge the Mechanical American, to a game of chess."

Thunder rumbles, outside. Or was it another gun shot? A camera operator shouts.

"Fuck this! I'm out!"

She bolts for the front door. A man in riot armor is following behind her. Grady yells.

"What are you doing, Riggs?!? You're *OUT* of the damn force if you…"

The door slams. The living room quiets. A green light blinks, above the latch. *Good.* Being alone all this time made Earl a lot meaner, but he didn't become cruel. He believes in second chances, which is what those two just got. The rest *chose* to stay here. Grady says.

"Fucking pussy! Whatever. Riggs was a disgrace to our uniform anyway!"

The other cop chuckles, but there's only two of them now. The odds are even. Earl asks.

"Does *anyone* in here have the guts to challenge my friend?"

Grady heaves, throws his legs up, and finally flings himself out of the recliner. He says.

"I can beat whatever monkey is hiding out in that machine. Let's go!"

And walks to the oak desk. Grady sits, across from the Mechanical American. Earl says.

"Very good. The pieces are already in place. My friend plays white, so he goes first."

Gears clank. The statue's left arm is reaching for a pawn. He's quick, but Grady yells.

"Fuck that! I'm an Officer of the Law, so *I* get to go first!"

Maybe he doesn't like being black. Grady moves an onyx pawn up two spaces, before the statue can finish his first move. Metal groans. It's a new, painful note. The Mechanical

American shakes his hideous, melted head. He grabs Grady's pawn, then moves it back to its original place.

The living room is still, until the sound lady laughs. The lighting guy does too.

The big cop's jaw is turning red. Is it about to burst? Earl asks.

"What's wrong? You read about this *hoax*! Don't you remember what happens, when his challengers make illegal moves? Hell, a lot of them tried, but even *Napoleon* backed down!"

Flashing lights burst, from the corner of Earl's eye. He looks right. He sees his reflection on his wall, but it's no mirror. There's rolling text, on the bottom of the screen.

"*SUSPECT WHO FLED SHOOTING CAUGHT IN HIS OWN HOME!*"

So, *PIGS* chose Earl, for tonight's live *punishment*. How fitting.

The statue picks up a white knight, and jumps it over its pawns. Grady says.

"Yeah, yeah, yeah. I read *all* about it. Tell me, what happened to Napoleon again?"

He moves the Mechanical American's horse back to its original place, and adds.

"That's right, he fucking *lost*! Guess what, Earl? That's not me. *I* am the law, not this fucking machine! And if *I* decide that the black team goes first? That's what happens! Got it?!?"

"*CHECK!*"

Uh-oh. The Mechanical American is getting angry. Grady is too. Earl says.

"Let him go first, Grady. *Trust me*, I'm trying to do you a favor."

"You know what I think about you and your *favors*, old man?"

Grady reaches across the chess board, picks up the white queen, and adds.

"I think you're nothing but *ARGHHH*!!!"

Earl smiles. The Mechanical American just seized Grady's arm.

The big cop screams, and thrashes around in that chair, but the statue's grip is strong. The crew gasps. The other cop bolts up, but Earl opens the coffin, hits a red button inside, and says.

"Oh, it's *way* too late for that now…"

Metal screeches. Loud crashes come next. The barbarians dart their heads, side to side. Iron shutters just dropped over every window in this living room, and the rest of Earl's house.

He hears a thud. Footage on the wall spins. They all run for the front door, but the visor gets there first. He grabs the latch. There's a sizzle, and a scream. He should've looked down. The handle is glowing red. Smoke rises, while panic erupts. Earl hasn't grinned like this in years.

The statue doesn't need power. The small, coffin-like box was always a trick, so Earl rigged up the switch for his *OH SHIT* home defense program in there instead. It worked.

"LET ME GO, MOTHERFUCKER!"

"*CHECK! CHECK!*"

Grady is thrashing around like a bull, but he's stuck. The Mechanical American tightens his grip around Grady's arm. Earl hears a *SNAP*. The gauntlet breaks in two, like a toy bracelet. Flesh below crunches, with bone. But Grady doesn't scream. He looks into the statue's eyes, and stops resisting. He just stares, into those hollowed out caverns. What's he seeing in there?

The Mechanical American uses his other hand to sweep all the chess pieces off the board.

Glass shatters. Earl sees a bright flash. *POP! POP! POP!* Firecrackers burst, over his purple carpet. Chemicals gave the chess pieces their colors, and they don't react well to oxygen. Flames spread fast, across his living room. It's full of old, wooden junk. Dusty books, stacks of yellowed newspapers. His wife once called it a *tinderbox*. That was the whole idea.

The other barbarians are scurrying around, helpless. Just like D'Angelo was. Earl yells.

"Get used to the heat, boys! There's *a lot* more of that, where *YOU* fuckers are going!!!"

They all scream, except Grady. Lettuce snaps. The Mechanical American is still crushing the big cop's wrist, but he remains still. Even as flames start consuming them both, Grady keeps staring into those eyes. Earl *could* walk over to his favorite recliner, plop down, and watch nature work wonders, but there's a glowing red light on the floor. He looks directly into the camera, and America. Everyone is watching. Earl saved up a lot, over the years. He unloads it all.

"Do *you* remember D'Angelo Watkins? He was my son, but I saw Dee get murdered on *PIGS*, just like you. Over and over again. They shot him thirty nine times that night. For what? For *you*. My wife couldn't take the pain. The gossip. The replays. I've been alone in this house, for ten long years. But you *loved* the blood, didn't you?"

Earl coughs. It's hot. Smoke is getting thick in here, but he keeps talking.

"Do you still love it now? No? Oh well. *These thugs should've complied*!"

Earl looks up, and stares at Dee's picture. His son's smile is beaming down. He feels tears, finally flowing down his cheeks. *I love you, Dee.* His son's grin seems to be widening, before flames shoot up between them. The camera is gone, swallowed by the blaze. It's time.

Earl stomps on the stained carpet. His gut drops. Air rushes through his ears. Heat fades. He's falling, just like he planned, if this day ever came. He lands on a big cushion, but it still hurts. It's dark and cool down here. Earl darts his head around the sub-basement, and listens.

Sirens shriek, outside. Grady's back-up is arriving. What took them so long? Everyone in America just saw what happened. Earl waits for their usual, oppressive racket, but glass shatters instead. It sounds like a brick just flew through a windshield. Shouting comes next.

"Fuck off, pigs!"

"GET THE HELL OUTTA HERE!!"

"Dee sent us, bitches!"

Earl smiles. Maybe *PIGS* isn't as popular as everyone thought it was. He settles into his hiding place. It's well-supplied. No one else but him even knows that this sub-basement exists.

He'll let everyone think that he's dead, for now. *The martyr's last stand* is an easy story to sell. Even when Grady's friends show up to investigate, and can't find Earl's body in the charred wreckage, they'll just pretend that they did. They'll *want* to believe that Earl is gone.

But he'll be out there, waiting. Watching, planning his next moves.

The Mechanical American will be too. Earl should've built him a shelter, but the statue wanted it this way. A typed note appeared on his desk this morning, like they always did. It said: *"After the third burn, I'll finally be free."* Earl's ears perk up. His friend is still shouting, upstairs.

"CHECK! CHECK! CHECK!"

ORANGIE AND THE GATES

Orangie sprints down a narrow tunnel. Trains rumble above. Muck splashes below.

THUD.

The booming noise echoes across the concrete tube, like a big, ominous drum.

It's a reminder. Orangie is late for work. Real late. He keeps running.

Black and white trash bags are waving, all over the tunnel. They're banners, for politicians. It's election night. Each color is a choice. *Change*, or *stay the course*.

"Vote for Pizza!"

"Fuck that! Choose violence! We need Whiskers!"

Activists are yelling. Their passion makes sense. Orangie is angry too, like every other rat in the city. Things haven't been going so good for them lately.

"But Pizza keeps us..."

THUD.

The noise silences the activists, for now. But it won't last long. Tonight's election is *all* about the Gates of Avalon. Orangie is one of the rats who sits on them, and he still doesn't know how he's going to vote. He stops by a metal grate, and pants outside of work.

THUD.

The noise rattles his guts. It's coming from inside of that grate, but it isn't a drum. Things are *knocking* in there. Pounding on gates that should never be opened. Strange, terrible monsters.

They're ancient, and angry. They've wanted to escape for a long, long time.

But luckily, for humans, rats like Orangie sit on the Gates of Avalon. It's their sacred purpose. Gates that should never be opened grow where humans flourish, and rats keep them shut. It's why they always follow big groups of people. It's how things have always been done.

But not if Whiskers wins tonight.

Orangie keeps panting, outside of the grate. He's in the basement of a buried tunnel, but this opening leads to a sublevel, even deeper below. He collects himself, then walks into work.

THUD.

Rookies cover their ears, but Orangie knows it won't help. Everything is louder in here. This chamber is a pit. A collection point. The ceiling is taller than a grand cathedral, too tall to comprehend. The floor is a crater, made of human failures. It's a slope of trash, copper pipes, marble, concrete, and lumber. All shredded, bent, and cracked. It's debris from structures that humans built, on the land above this pit. It spans many eras, that ended in collapse. Humans call it *bad luck.* They whisper about the location being *cursed.* They have no idea.

Orangie hops between plastic and diapers. He's heading for the hatches, at the bottom of the crater. He's two hours late, but no one yells at him. Marshall's gold toilet is empty. *Wow.* His boss didn't even show up today. Do they have the same excuse? Probably. Orangie can't sleep. He can't stop thinking about his family, and everyone else that he's lost. He isn't alone. *A lot* of rats have died lately. He can see it when he looks at the Gates of Avalon.

THUD.

Ancient hatches are bumping, up and down. Pressure from below is forcing them open, in cracks. Like the lid of a neglected, boiling pot. Hundreds usually sit on the gates. A collective weight, to keep them sealed. Not now. There *might* be fifty rats on duty today. Maybe. It shows.

THUD.

Orangie gulps. It's never been *this* loud. Can the beasts below smell weakness? Do they think their time is finally here? Why wouldn't they? The Gates of Avalon have never been this light. The hatches grew out of rocks, at the bottom of this crater. They're made of ancient, ornate metal. Humans wouldn't recognize the alloy, because it's older than humans. It's strong, but the gates can only contain those below with added pressure, and there aren't many sitters left. Too many died. Volunteers dried up. To most rats, Orangie, and those who still show up are either heroes, or fools. There's no middle ground, and opinions are hardening. Cruelty is trending.

All because of humans. With their typical *wisdom*, and flagrant hypocrisy, they declared war on rats. Again. *Because they serve no natural purpose.* Why do people hate them so much? Would the idiots change, if they knew about these gates? No. Humans love hatred, and killing. They always come up with new ways to *eradicate* rats, but this time, it's actually working.

Their new toxin is invisible. It sticks to food, and only kills rats, so the sweaty idiots are spraying it everywhere. Rats can't smell it. Even Orangie, and his nose is better than most. He missed it last week, and saw it poison his whole family, at once. The toxin works fast, but death comes slow. Real slow. Slow enough to turn a good heart cruel. Too many lives have been lost.

It's why the Gates of Avalon are creaking open, and Orangie keeps getting triple shifts. Everyone who still shows up for gate duty is bone-tired. It's almost funny. Most who've been killed in this chemical war were the rats who wanted peace with humans. All the calm, rational voices in this city's great mischief are vanishing. Those that remain are neither calm, or rational.

Do the sweaty idiots even know what they're stirring up? Orangie thinks about Pizza. She's the mascot of this troubled status quo. She became their leader, after humans filmed her dragging a cheese slice down subway stairs. It went *viral.* They called her *Pizza Rat*, but most just call her Pizza. She said that her fame was proof that humans and rats could live in peace.

It worked, for a dozen terms. Usually, when election time comes around, her black banners fly uncontested. But things are changing. In this election, Pizza has a challenger.

Whiskers, and his white bag party, have a different plan. He wants rats to retaliate against humans, abandon their posts, and let the monsters below open the Gates of Avalon.

It's a wild idea. One that was previously unthinkable. For Orangie, at least.

Whiskers has *always* wanted to open them. He's a consistent extremist, but he was a minor politician. His following was small. A joke. Not now. The madness of the world has caught up with the madness of Whiskers. Friendly rats are angry, and the angry are emboldened. *Fringe* ideas are now mainstream. Whiskers turned the Gates of Avalon into the main issue of tonight's election. If Pizza wins, the gates will stay closed. But if Whiskers wins?

All bets are off.

Orangie scales a styrofoam ramp, and climbs onto the ancient hatches. He plops next to another sitter, but doesn't look at them. He's too tired for greetings, or small talk. They are too.

THUD.

Orangie bounces up and down, on hard, ornate metal. It hurts. When the gates were fully staffed, these tremors were minor. The pain was manageable.

"OW! FUCK!"

His neighbor is also having a hard time. She must be new. But her teeth don't smell white. They're yellow. She's old. *Seasoned*, like Orangie. *Wow.* His neighbor is a volunteer.

They haven't had one of *those* in a while. He asks.

"Are you crazy? Or stupid?"

"Ex-*CUSE* ME?!?"

Orangie smirks. He's got a live one after all. He says.

"Sorry…It's just been a while since we've had a new volunteer. I forgot my manners. I should've said: *What the hell is wrong with you?*"

The neighbor laughs. A little too hard. She didn't answer his question either. She asks.

"What do *you* think will happen, if we let them open the gates?"

Her voice sounds vaguely familiar, but Orangie can't place it. He replies.

"I don't know."

And shrugs. It's the truth. No one knows what will happen. *THUD.*

But that relentless pounding is telling, about the beasts below. They take what they want, and destroy the rest, just like humans. Maybe the two should finally meet. His neighbor says.

"Maybe it won't be so bad, if we let them open the gates. For *us*, I mean. The prophecies say it'll be certain doom for humans, but they don't mention *us*! We're *survivors*!"

Survivors. What a word. A wave of numbness washes over Orangie. From the tip of his red nose, to the points in his claws, all the way down to the bottom of his tail. He stares at bent, faded patterns on the hatches below. *Pretty.* The neighbor sniffs, and gasps.

"Shit! I'm so sorry! You just lost your family. I can smell it on you."

Orangie sighs. He doesn't want pity. He just wants to die. *THUD*.

Sulphuric wind is leaking out of cracks in the gates. It smells like evil, in its purest form.

"And you're right. This *is* my first day down here. Am I *that* obvious?"

Must be nice, Orangie thinks. But he asks.

"Why?"

"Why what?"

"Why the hell did you volunteer to come down here?"

"Didn't you?"

Orangie says nothing. The neighbor keeps talking.

"I had to escape my hole, and my head. I lost my family too. Last week. I only survived, because I let the little ones eat my portion of our family dinner. They looked *so hungry*…"

She stares off into space. Orangie is pretty sure he still hates her, but now he understands her. She's suffering too. Bad. Maybe even worse than him. Enough to be happy to be here. To her, this turbulence is better. A mind must be quite cruel to itself, to make *this* seem appealing.

Orangie knows the feeling. Tears are brewing, behind his eyes. He also survived, because he let his kids eat his cut of their family dinner. *They looked so hungry.*

He shouldn't be here. He should be with his family, in the mythical rat city of food.

THUD.

But here he is, crashing into metal. All to protect the humans, who just killed his family. Orangie is too damn selfless. Why should he sit on these gates? Deep down, he knows. He's seen humans who like rats, and rats who like humans. They don't have to be enemies. Hell, they need each other. If the gates open, ecosystems will collapse. Food will get scarce, and *a lot* worse.

"You know the funny part? I used to stick up for humans. I took a lot of shit for it too, but my daughter loved them. No matter what those big, sweaty idiots did, she said: *Don't hate them, they don't know any better.* But she's dead now, because of humans. You think they *don't* know about these gates? C'mon! They go to the fucking moon! They know, they just don't care."

THUD.

"Maybe we're sitting on the answer, to all our problems! Maybe Whiskers is right! Maybe we *should* just get up and leave!"

Orangie says nothing. The idea sounded crazy in the past, even evil. But now? It almost sounds *fun*. His wife and his little ones aren't here to remind him, about the nice things in life.

"Or maybe I'm just nuts. What do you think? How are *you* gonna vote tonight?"

Orangie looks down. It's a good question. Watching all those unsuspecting humans suddenly learn how critical rats have always been, to their *civilization*? It would be cathartic, maybe even healing. He shouldn't do it, but he *wants* to. He knows that Whiskers is a maniac. And when his family was still alive, his decision would've been easy. But now? Orangie says.

"I have no idea."

And finally looks at the skeptic that's been sitting next to him. Holy shit. It's Pizza Rat.

Shock washes over Orangie, like a splash of cold water. Something snaps, deep within. He hears loving voices, from a city far away. Resolve starts burning again. He shouts.

"C'mon now, Pizza! Enough! You're our leader! You can't do this! *We* can't!"

She glares back, furious. Their spoiled secret is causing a stir. Other sitters on the gates are whispering now, and staring between them. Orangie keeps yelling.

"I *want* to get up, and let them all burn, just like the rest of you! But what are we gonna do about food, when the humans are gone? Huh?!? What will we eat?"

Pizza frowns, but she's thinking about it. Others nod. Is the tide turning? Maybe. If Orangie keeps this up, maybe they can rally together, and defeat Whiskers. A new voice yells.

"Did someone say *food*?!?"

Orangie turns. His boss finally showed up. Marshall drags a box of donuts onto the Gates of Avalon. Orangie runs over. He starts feasting, before thinking. Pizza does too. Strawberry, with sprinkles. It's delicious. Orangie forgot how hungry he was. They all did. Then he coughs.

So does Pizza. It spreads to the others. Shit. He heard this same raspy cough, after his kids ate that cursed family dinner. Breathing gets harder, but everything else gets easier. The gates are thudding below. Fuck it. Orangie is limp, and bouncing around, but he feels no pain.

The Gates of Avalon are finally opening.

WHERE DO THEY GO?

The sun is shining across a crowded park. Trees are finally starting to bloom again. It's October 1st. Spring is here. Ted smiles. He's sweating, but he'll take it. The hologram terminals outside of the park gates read 101. It never stays crisp and cool like this for long. Soon it'll get scorching, or worse. The heatwave won't relent until fall returns, sometime in March.

Ted strolls. A wasp buzzes past, but it's probably made of metal. He hears birds, distant music, and laughter. It's his day off. Tomorrow, he goes back to the docks. He repairs the city's flood walls. He'll be welding holes, waist deep in dirty ocean water. That endless, bubbling tide. Debris and bodies, peppered with artifacts from the Before Times. Most of Ted's coworkers are robots. How much longer until they make him obsolete? What will he do then?

Fuck it. He's here now, and Ted has a plan to make his day in the park special.

Jackhammers erupt in his skull. He hears strange, whispered phrases behind them, like fragments of a dream. *Take me out to the ball game.* The melody is worse than usual. So is

this headache. He walks faster, or maybe he stops. *Life, Liberty,*

*and…*Salvation!

Up ahead, Ted sees a tall, glowing monolith.

All the grass around that hologram terminal is dead.

Even the dirt below is grey. He runs towards it. Drills in his head

fade, as he gets closer. Intrusive voices dim. But it'll all come

back, if Ted strays too far from this humming machine. It's

flashing. What's today's alert?

"ILLEGALS INVADING ALL OVER THE COUNTRY!"

Ted shrugs. What else is new? The grassy field ahead is

full of them.

"STAY VIGILANT! REPORT ALL *SUSPECTED*

ILLEGALS TO THE CSV!"

Ted looks at his phone. Pop ups taunt him. Spam and

scams are all he gets on this thing, but he flips it over, and smiles

at a sticker. It's President Hawthorne, Ted's only friend. He had a

family, once. Even some buddies. But they all hated the

President, and Ted couldn't associate with traitors. He blocked them, or worse. He salutes Hawthorne, then turns to the field ahead.

There's a festive crowd. They're sitting on blankets, sharing food, and laughing. It isn't a picnic. It's a banquet. Ted sees grapes, bananas, and bottles of cold, clear water. Is that cheese? They even have bread. Fuck. He can't afford these luxuries. Ted frowns. They don't look like him. They don't talk like him, and they're eating *his* fucking grapes.

One of them sees him watching, and waves. Ted smiles back, then texts the CSV tipline. Soon, he'll watch these happy groups scatter. CSV agents will make them *all* take The Test.

Ted doesn't know where those unmarked white vans take illegals, and he doesn't care.

"*PRESIDENT HAWTHORNE CAN ONLY PROTECT US, WITH YOU!*"

Their leader is pointing at Ted, from the hologram terminal. A buzz shoots past his face. He claps at the wasp, then his nose starts burning. A flash of sharp pain, with no smoke. Fucker. He just got stung. Then the music stops. The park gets quiet.

Even the birds quit chirping. Ted gulps. Oh shit.

There's a man with a clipboard, sitting on a bench. It's close, and he's waving. He has a square jaw, and an easy smile. Tan khakis, black shirt, and a white armband, with a glowing monocle over his right eye. Fuck. That uniform is infamous. Who is this CSV agent waving at?

Ted turns around, but there's no one behind him. Every illegal in the field is running.

"Yes, Ted Matheson! *You*!"

Shit. He turns back to that voice. The agent is glaring. Fuck. Ted has to take The Test.

Birds sing, above. A melody fit for a fool. This is all wrong. President Hawthorne won, by promising to evict every illegal in America, with the CSV. Ted didn't fear them, or their new powers. But he never thought that *he'd* have to take The Test. Why would he? He was born here. He's never left this country. How could anyone question his citizenship?

"Have a seat, Mr. Matheson."

That monocle flickers. The CSV agent pats an empty spot on the bench. Hammers thud, on Ted's left. It sounds like they're crashing into steel, until they start jabbing at his brain. *We hold these truths to be*…He stumbles, and looks up. Shit. The hologram terminal went dark. It's the only one in sight. Power drills shriek, upstairs. *The only thing we have to fear is*…Leaves rustle, ahead. Tall shapes emerge. Riot armor, black visors. It's CSV enforcers. The *bad cops*.

…*Fear itself.*

They have big, glowing rifles. Ted walks over to the bench, and sits next to the agent. The metal seat is hard and unforgiving. What the fuck? *Ted* called their tipline! He asks.

"Can I help you?"

"*SIR*, MR. MATHESON!!!"

Ted's mouth goes dry. The CSV agent is loud. He jots a short, bold note on his clipboard.

"You will address me as *SIR*! Do you understand?"

That monocle tilts upwards. The agent scowls. His eyes are grey meteors, racing into the atmosphere from an unknown dimension. Flickering in his skull, starting to ignite. Ted says.

"Yes, *sir*…"

But he's getting angry. Hawthorne created the CSV, and the President is on Ted's phone! He's been legal his whole damn life, and his taxes pay this asshole's salary! Fuck this. Ted adds.

"…But you *do* know that I'm an American citizen, right?"

"Oh, really? I've never heard *that* one before…"

The agent laughs, but Ted doesn't join in. He yells.

"Excuse me, *sir,* but this whole fucking field is *full* of illegals!"

The CSV agent's eyebrows rise. He looks side to side, and says.

"*What* other people, Mr. Matheson?"

Ted looks around the grassy field. Shit. He forgot. Everyone took off. Abandoned blankets and piles of luxury food are the only witnesses left. The agent adds.

"Are you calling me crazy, or do you think I'm stupid?"

He pulls a red marker out of his pocket. Fuck. He can do whatever he wants. Ted says.

"No, *sir,* I'm…"

"Ready to begin The Test? Very good, Mr. Matheson."

He's cornered. The Test is three questions long, but it isn't like the phantom song in his head. It isn't *three strikes and you're out*. If Ted gets *any* question wrong, he'll be declared an illegal, and get hauled away in a white van. Where do they go? *Now* he cares.

The agent licks his finger, and flips a page. His glowing monocle is humming. All CSV agents wear them. Ted sees small, running lines of code in that visor, but that's it. Is it a script? If so, what's the clipboard for? It's stacked with pages, and the agent is scanning them close. Yet, the monocle is doing *something*. What? No one knows, except the CSV. Grey meteors light up.

"What is the capitol of the United States of America?"

Ted exhales slow. So far, The Test is easy. He answers.

"Creede, Colorado."

"Not bad, Mr. Matheson."

The agent marks his clipboard, and turns the page. Ted hears a loud, droning beep.

A white van is backing up, too close. Sweat falls, and sizzles on his knee. He can't just show them a passport. Legal documents aren't good enough for the CSV. Ted knows. He voted for this. When Hawthorne said that random citizenship tests, from his agents, was the only way to evict every illegal, Ted agreed. Back then, he said: *"If you have nothing to hide, why worry?"*

Now he's trying not to fidget.

Hammers pound at his skull. Power drills join in. Intrusive voices are getting louder. Ted looks to his savior, but the tall monolith is still dead. *You better not pout, you better not cry...*

When did hologram terminals first appear? Ted vaguely remembers a time, long ago, when he didn't have to be near them all the time. But he was young. That was before the floods and fires got *real* bad. Before hundreds of millions became homeless. Before the War. And the next one. And the one after that. It was chaos. But Hawthorne brought order.

Didn't he?

The construction site in Ted's mind is levelled by an earthquake. He's far past dizzy. If he wasn't already sitting, he'd fall over. These headaches always get critical, when Ted tries to remember the Before Times. Why? Were hologram terminals built to wipe out all memories?

"Who was the first President of the United States of America?"

The agent is glaring. Bad cops are ready to swarm. *Use your credit card now*. No. Please. Not now. *Four score, and*...Fuck off! Shit. Did Ted just say that out loud? *Fuck off* isn't the first President, but the man with a monocle grunts. He's still waiting for an answer. Ted blurts out.

"Henry Ford!"

"*President* Henry Ford, Mr. Matheson!"

Ted's whole body clenches up, like he tripped in a dream. Is this it? Did he fail The Test?

"But I'll allow it."

The CSV agent's easy smile returns. For how long? Ted gulps. Years ago, a pundit he hated warned that eventually, the CSV would come after *everybody*, even Hawthorne voters like Ted. But he didn't listen, even when that same pundit was called a terrorist, and hauled away on camera. But whatever. Fuck him. There's only one question left. The others were common

knowledge, *historical facts*. Maybe Ted is safe. But then he gets
an idea. A damn good one.

"Wait a minute, can't I just give you a character
reference?"

Camera shutters flicker over the grey meteors. The CSV
agent says nothing. Ted goes on.

"Like a friend, or a family member? Someone who'll tell
you that I am who I say I am?"

The agent's expression remains blank, but buried
somewhere deep within, a smirk might be growing. Or maybe
it's a snarl. He says.

"*Fine*, Ted. Who should I call?"

The agent spoke like a coiled rattlesnake, but Ted is
euphoric. *You're a genius*! He starts turning through names in his
mind, cards that fit the bill. But he keeps tossing them aside.
Jokers. Duds. Each one has been *blocked*, usually by Ted. Others
got hauled away. Friends and family. All because of Hawthorne.
His best friend. The President. Shit. The last card is a joker. Ted's
hope pops, like a balloon. An empty void is all that's left. Who
can he call? The agent says.

"That's what I thought. Don't interrupt me again."

Grey meteors in his skull are engulfed with flames. They're close to the planet's surface. Chunks are breaking off. The collision will be devastating. An extinction level event. Maybe Ted isn't imagining the fire. The CSV agent says.

"Last question. What right does the second amendment give to the American people?"

Ted laughs. *Really*? That's it? This is easy. For once, all of his strange, intrusive thoughts line up with the *correct* ones. Why is everyone so afraid of The Test? Fucking cowards. He says.

"The right to bear arms."

Ted grins. He did it. He really…

"*WRONG*, Mr. Matheson!"

What the fuck? The tall monolith is flashing again. The CSV agent keeps yelling.

"The second amendment gives *the police* the right to bear arms! That's how it's *always* been, here in the United States of America! But an *illegal* like you wouldn't know much about our Constitution, now would they?"

Ted's headache is gone, but the hammers and drills are getting louder. Big, cold hands grab him, from all sides. Something sharp pierces his neck. His body goes limp. He can't move, but he isn't numb. Hard, icy hands lift him away from the park bench. Why are they so cold?

Hammers thud. Drills whirr. The noises are rhythmic, like marching footsteps. Ted feels his work boots sliding across the grass. Enforcers are dragging him towards a white, unmarked van. It's waiting in the shadows, between tall trees. But Ted gets an idea. A damn good one.

The President can get him out of this! If *anyone* can, it's him! Ted's his biggest fan! His phone has a sticker of Hawthorne's face! Isn't that enough proof? Ted tries to shout, but the words are stuck. His throat is numb. It won't even whimper. The van is getting closer.

Somewhere in the distance, music starts playing again.

FAMOUS GREMLINS

Lucinda stops slurping. She's satisfied with her bath, for now. Hard grey walls surround her, but stars are shining above. The hunter stretches her orange legs, and extends her sharps.

Wind howls, beyond the concrete pit. But it's warm down here. Giants call it a *foxhole*.

It's deep, like a shallow grave, and wide enough for two giants. They visit this pit during the day, and pose in here. Square, consuming windows *capture the moment*. The paved foxhole is a *tourist attraction*, but now, it's secluded. Lucinda only bathes alone. She lives in a tank, but tonight, it had *visitors*. She came down to this pit for privacy, but it makes her uneasy.

Her sharps can't pierce these walls. There's only one way out, and hunters like options.

Lucinda squats, then leaps out of the foxhole. An easy jump, for a hunter like her. Cold wind howls through trees, and cuts across a manicured lawn. It's littered with jeeps, cannons, and other rusted war machines. Their barrels are metal eyes, with caverns for pupils. They have no purpose, or enemy. They're retired. Giants left them out here, in the garden of their museum.

It's crowded tonight. Tall trees anchor both sides of the paved foxhole, like guards. Wide trunks. Bare, skeletal limbs. The cottonwoods match. Are they twins? Their branches stretch out, all the way to the top of this hill, and a big granite wall. It's a *monument*, full of chiseled letters.

"Hey!"

A winged foe startles her. A dark one. Lucinda knows her. Sarah keeps talking.

"Why aren't you in your house, *Tank Cat*?"

"You know why, Sarah. You're *their* fucking chaperone tonight, aren't you?"

The crow stares, ahead. She's tense. Sarah is hosting the shape's *gathering*. She squawks.

"Relax, *Loosie*! It's only…"

Something whistles past Lucinda's head. She jumps back. Wings flap, above. Sarah shot up quick, to dodge that rock. She's fast too. A voice calls, from uphill.

"Fucking *bird*! Get the hell outta here! I'm trying to think!"

Frost crunches below. Lucinda runs into a bush, and peeks between sticks and leaves. Her pupils shrink, to vertical slits. There's a giant at the top of this hill. He shivers, in a long black raincoat, while waiting by the solemn granite wall. He threw that rock. *Bad call, champ.*

Fog grows, over the monument. Chiseled names are glowing, under the moonlight. Is the giant a *businessman*? He has their standard, leather briefcase, except it's handcuffed to his wrist. Metal jangles, behind him. Like shaking keys. But he doesn't hear it. He thinks that no one else is out here. Is Lucinda jealous? She sees things that giants can't. And this garden is *bustling*.

Shapes are everywhere. They move like mist, drifting in and out of this dimension. Dented helmets, torn fatigues. Tired faces, from many eras. Some resemble giants. Others are static clouds. Lucinda keeps her distance. They aren't interested in her either. She hears bits of their stories, as they murmur past. They talk of pawns and puppets, and debts that must be paid.

The shapes point at the business giant, and whisper like he's famous. He mutters.

"Get it together, Byron…"

Lucinda settles in. *Hello, Byron.* She loves drama, and giants are quite good at it. They reveal a lot, when they think that no one is watching. And this one is restless. There's a heavy object in his pocket. It's making his pants sag, and radiating bad energy. Hunters can see many possible futures, if they stare at any item long enough, and that one is a *magnet*, for dark futures.

And yet, Byron always keeps it close. It makes him feel safe. Giants are strange animals.

He turns to a trailer hitch, parked by the granite wall. It's a flat steel bed, holding six big, pointed tubes. Each one is long, and wide enough to swallow an oil barrel. They make fire. All six are stacked together, like cigarettes in a pack. They're aiming at the sky. Lucinda winces.

White orbs flash, at the end of a long road. Byron tenses up. He knows these headlights. They pull around a corner, and vanish into trees. Leaves rustle, above. It's winter. Why haven't they fallen? The fog grows taller, and thicker. A door closes. She hears footsteps, as Byron yells.

"Fred! Are you outta your fucking mind?!?"

"Maybe I am, Byron. Maybe I am."

A new giant emerges, from the shadows. Tall, gaunt, and wearing a white coat. It must be Fred. Grey, frazzled hair. Haunted, greedy eyes. He's tired, but alert. He doesn't sleep much, like Byron. They both fear the realm that awaits, behind their eyelids. He stops near Byron, who asks.

"If you leak this blueprint, do you have *any* idea how many people are going to die?"

Fred laughs. It echoes, under the monument. The wall full of names. Byron screams.

"You think this is *funny*?!?"

Lucinda's ears flicker. Keys are jangling, all over the garden. The noise is coming from everywhere, and nowhere. Do the giants hear it? Fred catches his breath, and speaks.

"We had quite a system, didn't we? We even had a code name. *Gremlins*. The military contracted your company, to invent new toys. I made them, then met you out here, for *tweaks*.

Armor, launchers, bomb detecting wands. We broke my creations, to make more money."

Lucinda shuffles, on the pile of dead leaves. *Gremlins.* It's a fitting name. Fred adds.

"Troops blamed the *accidents* on small, mythological critters. Our predecessors taught us well. If everyone is gossiping about gremlins, then no one asks who made all their shitty gear."

Byron grins. He's proud of their work. Fred goes on.

"But we didn't just waste money, did we? Have you ever wondered how many soldiers got killed by our *faulty* equipment, over the years?"

The jangling stops. The shapes are still. They're waiting. Listening close. Fred asks.

"No? Did you ever stop to think about what our *arrangement* was doing, to *me*?"

Lucinda shivers. Icy tension is building, all around. Fred snorts, and yammers on.

"I thought not. Building things made me proud, ever since I was a kid. But that wasn't what we did out here, was it? You humiliated me, for decades. But I won't ruin my work anymore. Not this time. The instant rifle is my masterpiece, and now, the world will finally…"

"But you *can't* leak it, Fred!"

The giants shuffle. Scowls deepen, but Byron is also starting to smirk. He adds.

"Did it hurt, when a simple password locked you out? I bet. I saw you obsess over Banalco's 3-D printed combat rifle, so I did what I had to do, to protect *my* blueprint!"

"And yet, I still have it."

Fred reaches into his pocket, and pulls out a small plastic box. Byron exclaims.

"C'mon! This is nuts! You want to give this rifle away, to *everyone*? Do you have *any* idea how many wars you'll start? I don't. *No one* does! But it'll be A LOT, I can tell you that!"

Fred spits on the pavement, below the monument.

"Save your lies for the press. You only care about money. And you just want to stop me, because I'm going to give away the blueprint for *my* instant, 3-D printed combat rifle, *for free*!"

Byron shudders. Lost profits haunt him, unlike blood, death, and tears. A tongue clicks.

"*Putting more weapons into the hands of more people will make all people safer*. You taught me that, Byron! You said it, for decades, but *I* live up to our principles! That's why I need to do this! Don't you see? *Everyone* will have equal access to deadly force! It'll protect us all!"

Lucinda tenses up, in the bush. Fibers are unravelling, below. Dead leaves will soon crunch, and a hunter never gives away their position. She darts down the frosty lawn. The tall cottonwoods are close. Their branches stretch out, all the way to the top of the hill.

"Are you *really* afraid of all those wars, Byron? Why? *Think of the profits*!"

Lucinda leaps, with her sharps out. They dig deep into the cold, dry bark. She climbs.

"Yeah, yeah, yeah, Fred. Cut to the chase, and call me a hypocrite. Feel better yet?"

Shapes murmur, all over the garden. The gremlins are fighting, but can they both lose? Nice giants found Lucinda, living in a rusted Sherman. They took care of her. They even called her *Tank Cat*. She owes them, and if these gremlins aren't stopped, *a lot* of giants will die. Too many. Lucinda halts. She was moving on auto-pilot. She didn't think, she just went.

Now she's dizzy, in a tall tree. Perched on the farthest end of a long branch. It's a dark limb, with many fingers. She's right above the wall, and those rockets. Everything below looks small. Wind blows across the garden, and up this tree. Her branch leans, and groans, but doesn't snap. Yet. Lucinda crawls forward, closer to the edge of the diving board. Fred says.

"Fine. Let's cut a deal. I'll destroy the blueprint."

Eyes bulge, in Byron's skull. Fred keeps talking.

"If you *really* think this printed rifle is evil, I'll stomp out the only copy of it, right now. That way, no one can have it. Crisis averted, with my integrity preserved. What do you say?"

Textures appear, in the bark below Lucinda. The garden brightens. Clouds drift, away from the moon. A black sky shifts, to a dark blue. It reveals many things, that giants can never see. If these two could, they'd run, deep into the woods. But they think they're all alone out here.

"That's it? Nothing? My printed rifle must be important to you too. Why else would you ignore your last chance to stop it, before it spreads? Guess it can't be *that* dangerous, huh?"

Latches pop. The briefcase is opening. Fred yells.

"Whoa, *partner*! If it's money in there, I'll stop you right now. Not even…"

Then gets quiet, when he sees what's inside. Why? Lucinda hears keys, right behind her. Shit. Something followed her, onto this branch. Few creatures can sneak up on a hunter. It's fast, and weightless. It isn't any animal she knows. She should jump, but curiosity makes her turn.

"*Whoa,* Byron! How generous! I'm honestly impressed, you old cheap-skate!"

Fuck. It's mist, with a dented helmet. A static cloud, shaped like a giant. They whisper. Metal jangles, over a torn uniform. It's a chain. *Oh*. She didn't hear keys. It was *dog-tags*. Every shape has these rattling necklaces. It's a weird name for giants to give to their own ornaments, but they keep whispering. They tell her a story, about Byron and Fred. She learns why the others are so excited, to see these famous gremlins. The shape points, below. Oceans of possible futures light up. She sees what happens if she does nothing. But she also sees glory. It seems too easy.

"You've got a deal, Byron!"

Something coughs. It's big, old, metallic, and grumpy. The contagion spreads, all over the garden. The gremlins shut up. *Now* they're listening. Rumbling, gravelly stomachs scream.

A bright glare comes next. Everything turns white.

Ivory fades to yellow, then pink. Lucinda blinks. Vertical pupils shrink to slits. Contours return, with definition. Spotlights are blasting at Byron and Fred, from all sides. She sees every little blemish and wrinkle. Long, cavernous eyes are sticking out, between the headlights.

Every dormant war machine in this garden just came back to life. Those engines *coughed*, while they were starting up. Now they're chugging, all over. A sour stink grows thick in the air. Diesel fumes mix with the fog. It's trapping their exhaust. Lucinda hears a snap, deep within the branch that she's perched on. Just like the shape said that she would. It's time.

She leaps off the diving board, and lands on a hard, frosted lawn. It hurts, but Lucinda keeps it moving. She's close to the granite wall. It's loud down here. Shrill, piercing. Rusted barrels, torrents, and cannons are moving, across the garden. Even her house joined the party. The Sherman has a new purpose. Like every other museum retiree out here, it's aiming at the gremlins. To them, it looks like *invisible hands* are guiding these machines. Not to Lucinda.

"What the fuck is this?!?"

"Nice try, Byron; but *c'mon*! It's your robotics division. It has to be."

"*You're* the one who was obsessed with *nano-possession*, remember?"

Why aren't they blaming it on *gremlins*? Lucinda thumps her tail, then leaps up in fright.

"Whatever, Byron! You know how old those fucking things are? There's no way that…"

BOOM!

A fireball erupts, across the garden. Lucinda sees flying dirt. It startles her, just like the thing that she hit with her tail. It was a metal box, with plastic switches. She pressed one of them.

"C'mon, Fred! Over here! *QUICK*!"

The giants take off running. They sprint right past Lucinda, towards the paved foxhole. It's tiny, and deep enough for two. Gears keep clanking, from all sides. Long eyes are following Byron and Fred. The famous gremlins think that a tank just fired at them, but it was a mine.

They dive into that shallow pit. Rusted barrels halt. The garden quiets. Almost.

"*AHH*!"

"What?"

"You broke it! The fucking blueprint!"

"NO WAY! That was all…"

Something cracks, like a bone. Lucinda looks up. The branch that she leapt from falls.

A crash echoes, across the garden. That big limb landed on the trailer hitch, and its cradle of rockets. Bolts snap. Metal folds. Dirt starts rumbling, below. Fuck. Something *big* is coming, downhill. It's an avalanche. A rolling force of nature, but it isn't snow. It's an object.

Long, tan, and wide enough to swallow an oil barrel. The missile rolls past her hiding spot. Five others are tumbling, close behind it. All heading downhill, towards the paved foxhole.

THUD! The first one slams into twin cottonwood trunks. They stop it cold, like a brick wall. Leaves fall, with twigs. *THUD*! *THUD*! *THUD*! Old trunks groan, but hold firm. One by one, the other silo tubes are piling up behind the first, like lemmings. The garden quiets. *Whoa.*

All six rockets are wedged, right above the paved foxhole. Byron and Fred are trapped in there. Boxed in, from above. They scream accordingly, but it's all muffled. Did the gremlins just realize how their deaths will be marked? *A freak accident, due to faulty equipment.*

"Don't you have somewhere to be, *Tank Cat*?"

Sarah is squawking above. Lucinda replies.

"Fuck off."

And gets up. The ground is hard. It's getting cold, and the fog is growing, but Lucinda knows of a spot, with a view. It's safe. She trots down frosted grass, and climbs into her Sherman tank. The same shapes are still in here. They're watching the show, through narrow steel hatches.

Lucinda hears their murmurs. *Oh.* This used to be *their* tank. Her stomach growls. Shit. After all that, she forgot about dinner. A shape kicks, below. She hears a hiss, and looks down. *Whoa.* A hatch opens. It's full of cans. The *rations* are old, but they haven't gone bad. The shape apologizes about their quality, but she scoops one out, pops it open with her sharps, and feasts.

The hunter purrs. Lucinda needs another bath, but it can wait. She keeps watching the six tombstones, with her brand new friends.

LAZDA

Lazda wakes up to a burst of pain. Her head just smashed into metal. She flies sideways. Her shoulder crashes into a wall. It's like she's trapped in a dryer. Where is she?

It's dark. It gets even darker when she opens her eyes.

She hears a loud, rumbling engine. Tires screech. *Oh.*

Lazda was sleeping on a bench in Santa Fe. The town square was empty. The moon was full. It was hanging low. A big, glowing eye. She didn't see any other homeless people. It was odd. She's lived outside, all over America. Usually, fellow campers are everywhere. But in that quiet mountain city, she was alone. It was alarming, but she drifted off on that hard metal bench, and thought that maybe it was because the city actually took care of its people. She was wrong.

Three men woke her up. They had black khakis, shiny boots, and white collared shirts. They looked like accountants, but their empty, excited eyes gave them away. Religious fanatics come in many flavors, but their eyes are all the same. A hollow, confident madness. The three men had matching batons, and leather bound books stamped with five gold letters. *JESUS.* But those bible pushers didn't talk to Lazda about hell, or even donations.

They asked if she wanted to play a game.

They offered her a thousand bucks. Lazda knew that a homeless woman in a tinfoil poncho would have to do something real fucked up to get money *from* bible pushers, but her stomach howled louder than reason. She said *yes*, and blacked out.

Now she's here. Lazda blinks. The abyss doesn't change.

She waves her hands. She can't see them, but they're moving. The bible pushers didn't tie her up, yet she's still in a cage. The floor rumbles below. Lazda sees shadows of her parents in the darkness. They're whispering in Latvian, about *Black Marias*.

Those dark, windowless Soviet vans had *fruit and vegetables* written on the side, but everyone knew what they really hauled. Black Marias always came in the middle of the night, along with hard, stomping boots. They made people disappear.

Struts groan below, like they're about to snap. Lazda must be in a vehicle. It's getting abused by the road. It feels like they're driving over dirt and rocks. Where are they going?

Lazda stretches in the dark. Her tinfoil poncho crinkles, like cheap wrapping paper. She wears this thermal blanket for good luck, but she's beginning to question its efficacy.

She checks her body for damage. Her joints, fingers, and toes are all moving. Nothing is broken, but dull pain in her head gets louder. How long was she out? It *could've* been days, but her nightmares had just started, when a head-on collision woke her up. Is dawn coming soon?

Where are they? If they drove south, they'll be in the middle of a desert by now. But if they went north, they could be deep in a forest. Anything is possible in New Mexico.

"What's her damage?"

"We've *never* had to work so hard to make a hobo take free money!"

"Well, it ain't *exactly* free…"

Unseen voices snort in agreement. Lazda knows them. It's the three bible pushers. What are they going to do to her? What *game* did she agree to play?

"Something is wrong with her."

Lazda smiles. They have no idea.

She comes from a long line of people who live outdoors. Mysterious outcasts. *Witches*.

Villagers feared her Oma, yet they ventured into her woods for medicine, and protection, when *real* monsters arrived. Her father was a Forest Brother. He fought Soviets, Nazis, then Soviets all over again. Her ancestors probably fought Crusaders too. All from the forest.

Oh yes. Something *is* wrong with Lazda. But she isn't like her ancestors. She might sleep outside, but she stays close to the village. After the sun goes down, she fears the forest. Oma told her stories about monsters who live in the trees. Beasts that eat people, and darken the land itself.

"That's why we're taking her to Dr. Irma."

After that, the men stop talking. Are they afraid? Who the fuck is Dr. Irma?

Howling gusts smack into the van. Distant coyotes shriek. Nails are scratching at the outer walls of her cage. Is it branches? Bones snap, under the tires. Or maybe it's twigs. Lazda sniffs, and smiles. It's moisture. A faint trace of humidity. So, they went north.

She made the same trip earlier today, to visit a forest. It was beautiful. Tall, pale spires were everywhere. All dotted with black spots. Latvians call them *berzs*. To them, birch trees are sacred. Each trunk is an outpost, a *limb* of the same giant, interconnected being.

And just like the villagers who came to her Oma when they were in trouble, Lazda is heading into the woods. The realm of strange, powerful beings. Gods, gnomes, shape-shifters, ghosts. She just hopes they avoid *the guardians*. Sumpurnis. Dogsnouts. Anything but them.

Lazda shuts her eyes, and shivers. She sees her Oma, flickering in a campfire.

Her gaunt, wrinkled face starts moving. Oma is talking, but Lazda can't hear her. Falling hooves are drowning her out. Loud, thundering, like falling artillery. Branches rustle, behind

Oma. Things are moving, deep in the woods. Far beyond the last flickers of light.

"Did you hear that?!"

"What are you talking about?"

"I *swear*, I just heard something, right behind us!"

"Shut up! Both of you! We're here!"

Lazda blinks. Oma and the campfire are gone. Shit. What did the bible pushers hear?

She gets thrown forward. Her head hits a wall, before she registers the screeching brakes. She lands on her tailbone, then the back door flies open. Lazda winces, from a punishing glare.

First, she sees dress shoes, khakis, and collared shirts. The three bible pushers are waiting outside the van, with iron clubs. Their books say *JESUS*, but their *real* gods are Greed and War. One is larger than the others. She'll call him Sugar Boots. He must've eaten the runt's food while they were growing up. His Lap Dogs gesture with their clubs, telling her to leave. Fuck it.

Lazda steps out of the van. She looks up, and sees branches. White bark is glowing, behind the men. Birch trees are towering above the van. She peers left. The pushers parked this Black Maria sideways, on a narrow dirt road. It carves a flat path through this mountain's slope.

The doors opened, by the edge of a cliff. If Lazda takes five steps past these men, she'll tumble down a steep hill. It's lined with legions of tall, pale trunks. They go on and on, skeletal and herd-like, flowing all the way down the side of this mountain, far as she can see. Lazda's ears perk up. She hears owls, but they aren't hooting. They're screaming. So are the crickets. The forest is loud tonight. It isn't their usual hits. Even leaves are shuffling, with pure, primal rage.

Why is everyone so angry? Lazda turns around, and gasps. Fuck.

The van's headlights are pointing at a field of stumps. Hundreds of them. They're casting long shadows. Each knee-high stump has white bark. Who cut them all down? The Black Maria is blocking half of the clearing from Lazda's view, but it's surrounded by evergreen trees. A fresh, haunted stink creeps up her nose. The massacre smells recent, but she finds a survivor.

One tree was spared, in the field of stumps. It looks lonely, around its fallen comrades.

Lazda squints. There's a sign hanging from its trunk. It's a picture of a parking lot. A promise of future glories, to be built on this graveyard. *Greedy, hideous fools.*

"Hey, bum! *I said*: MOVE IT!!!"

Sugar Boots is screaming, *way* too close to Lazda's face. She *could* hit him, but takes a deep breath instead. Lap Dogs start walking to the front of the van. She follows them, and asks.

"Why are you doing this to me?"

Sugar Boots looks confused, even insulted. He says.

"Our city is clean, and perfect. Everyone is cared for, until bums like *you* show up! You sleep outside, and stink up our streets. But it's ok. We're here to help you. It's our Holy Duty."

Lazda laughs. She can't help it. It's too much. She replies.

"So, Jesus told you to kidnap me?"

"He told me to do worse. But we didn't kidnap you. You *agreed* to play, remember?"

Lazda remembers the money, but she keeps playing dumb.

"Maybe I *want* to sleep outside. You ever think about that?"

"I don't need to think. Mental illness is a crime, and you're here to get cured."

Lazda shrugs. Why debate a cinderblock wall? She heard rumors about these laws, sprouting up all over America. They give militias the power to forcibly *hospitalize* anyone who's *having a psychiatric crisis*, which, in practice, means homeless people like Lazda. She asks.

"Where are we, Sugar Boots?"

"What the fuck did you just call me?!?"

The pusher narrows his eyes, and huffs like a bull. He loves his new nick-name. She says.

"*Your name*, Sugar Boots. I called you by your name. Have you forgotten it? Hmm, that's troubling. *Very* troubling indeed! Maybe *you're* the one who's having a psychiatric crisis!"

Lazda shakes her head. Sugar Boots scoffs, but his Lap Dogs start looking at him sideways. Studying him, suddenly unsure. Evergreens shake, at the edge of the clearing.

Something grunts. A big, unseen animal. What is it?

Lazda follows the noise, into the field of stumps. After she steps away from the van, she can see the rest of the clearing. Shit. There's a cabin, up ahead. A squat, wooden structure, that's painted black. Its windows are covered with yellowed newspapers. Who lives here? Is it one of these new *hospitals*?

CREAAAAK!

Fuck. That was a door. Lazda hears voices. A faint, impossible rabble, like thousands of people yelling at once. Grey squares emerge from the cabin. They're shining through the dark. Flickering, like static TVs. It's eyes, on a dark, human-like shape. Twigs snap. Shit.

It's moving fast, towards Lazda. Fuck. Glowing eyes, a shadow body, *and* it speaks with a thousand tongues? Is it one of Oma's monsters? The dark shape steps into the van's headlights.

A woman emerges. A tall, pale redhead, dressed in all black. It isn't the beast that Lazda envisioned, but her eyes really *are* glowing, like old TVs playing channel zero. Are they glasses?

"Welcome to the show, folks! I'm your host, Dr. Irma!"

Her face is tan, gaunt, and wrinkled. Her brow is severe, with a plastered-on smile. Sugar Boots and his Lap Dogs straighten their posture. The redhead must be their boss, but who is Dr. Irma talking to? The unseen rabble gets louder. They sound excited. Dr. Irma goes on.

"But before we begin, don't forget to ring that bell below, and hit subscribe!"

Lazda doesn't like where this is going. Dr. Irma is holding a duffel bag.

What was she doing in that cabin? She stares at Lazda, and frowns. Those lenses are mosaics, made of thousands of bright, tiny, honeycomb dots. What's in them? People?

Are those voices an *audience*? Dr. Irma lowers her glasses. Hard, empty eyes shift.

"What the…*AH*!!"

She taps the side of her glasses. Lenses darken, until they become clear. Then she yells.

"*That's* the best you could do? Really? This patient is pathetic! She'll be *way* too easy to cure! Her treatment will only last for a minute, tops! Another *boring* case like this will fuck my ratings, boys! Big time. How the hell do you idiots expect me to keep this hospital running!?!"

Lazda blinks. And they're saying that *she's* the crazy one.

Dr. Irma's tone is no longer bouncy, or melodic. It's cold, ruthless. She's being herself, while her audience is stuck on hold. She just humiliated three big men. Will one of them snap? They suck in air through their teeth, and lower their heads. Why do they cower to this woman?

Dr. Irma puts her glasses back on, and taps them. Lenses flicker, into an impossible rainbow of microscopic colors. Each individual honeycomb now looks like its own galaxy.

"Sorry about that, everyone! Fucking technical difficulties. *Help* these days, am I right?"

Dr. Irma is charming, while performing. Tiny voices erupt. Is it laughter? She goes on.

"Thank you for tuning in, and a big, special thanks to all of our generous patrons. Your donations keep my hospital running. And tonight, we have a *very* special patient for you!"

Dr. Irma turns to Lazda, looks her up and down like a shrewd casting agent, then adds.

"She smells even worse than she looks, folks! Delusional bums like this *used* to pollute our streets, before private treatment organizations like mine were finally allowed to help them! But luckily, my Holy Outreach Team found her, on a park bench. Now her cure can begin!"

Lazda sighs. *Private treatment organizations.* How Soviet. She looks at the cabin that Dr. Irma came from. Is it her *hospital*? Probably. Dr. Irma is tech-savvy. Those static glasses must be her camera, mic, and broadcast beacon. What kind of a fucked up *show* is this?

Judging from all those tiny voices, this woman attracts a crowd. What do they *pay* to watch, out here? Lazda learned a lot about America, from sleeping in her streets. She shudders.

Sugar Boots and his Lap Dogs have been to this cabin before. These woods are isolated, and the three bible pushers didn't argue about directions. They know what Dr. Irma does to her *patients*. It's bad enough to make them cower. Who is Dr. Irma? She's rich. Lazda can tell. It's all in her contempt. For them, and life in general. In that way, rich Americans and Soviet apparatchiks are quite similar. It's funny. Or maybe it isn't funny at all. Dr. Irma says.

"Now, let's get down to the…"

"Did you cut down those trees?"

Lazda points to the field of stumps. She loves interrupting *important* people. The pushers gasp, but Dr. Irma turns to the knee-high tombstones, and starts laughing. Loud. It echoes up the trees, and across the forest. Now they know *exactly* how she feels about their power. She says.

"*Interesting.* So, she's an environmentalist too! It figures. Yet *another* severe, untreated mental illness! This bum is in crisis. But we *all* know how to help her, don't we?"

Thousands yammer, with microscopic voices. Dr. Irma licks her lips. She's feeding from the frenzy she started, but the crickets shut up. So did the owl. The forest is listening. Lazda says.

"*I'd* be afraid, if I killed all those sacred trees."

The wind slows. Quiet comes next. It's ominous, and total, except for the van's chugging engine. Those headlights are still casting long shadows over the stumps. Dr. Irma shrugs.

"Are you ready to play the game?"

"What game? I thought you were going to *cure* me?"

"*I am*! Don't you get it yet, bum? The game *is* the cure!"

A stick breaks, somewhere beyond the circle of evergreens.

Dr. Irma turns. She waits, then chuckles. The pushers copy her, but it isn't convincing. *Do* they think it was nothing? Lazda listens. Mountain lions and bears are the least of their worries. Anything could be lurking, behind those trees. Wind howls. It's harsh, dusty. Branches groan, but Lazda feels a strange, familiar warmth in her chest. This is *her* turf. She says.

"You keep calling me *bum*. My name is Lazda."

"Look around, bitch! I own *all* of this land, for miles! I can do whatever the hell I want out here, so fuck your name! I'm gonna call you *rabbit*!"

Animals call, deep in the woods. Dr. Irma pivots.

"And now it's time to tell this rabbit the rules of the game!"

Melodic beeps erupt, from her glasses. Is it a strange, robotic form of applause?

"You get a two minute head start. That's it. *GO!!!*"

The wind slows. Leaves are still. Lazda's heart thuds, but she doesn't move. She asks.

"Where's my money, Irma?"

The redhead scowls. Good. Lazda won't dignify her fraudulent titles, or whatever *faith* she claims. Dr. Irma reaches down. Shit. What's in her duffel bag? She unzips it.

"What's wrong, rabbit? Too *lazy* to run? Wanna know what happens after two minutes?"

And pulls out something shiny. It's long. Stained, sticky, and shaped like an exclamation point. Dr. Irma runs her finger down it, revealing the silver edge of a blade. Shit. It's a machete.

Lazda runs. She's heading to the last place that *anyone* would want to go right now. She scales wooden steps, two at a time, and glides across a porch. A faint light is emanating behind old, yellowed newspapers. Fuck it. Lazda opens a door, and runs

inside Dr. Irma's cabin.

Her gut drops. A big stench ambushes her. It has thick,

overpowering, *complex* flavors. Rot, waste, decay. Burnt hair,

plastic. The stink has a personality. It's living, breathing, angry.

Her eyes short-circuit. Lazda stops running, but her feet

slide. She trips on something wet, and falls. Everything gets

dark. Or does it? She lands face-first. It feels like stale bread, and

rotten eggs. At least, she *hopes* it's spoiled food. Something

pops. A flood rushes into her mouth.

It isn't stale bread, or rotten eggs. Lazda coughs, and

thrashes around. She's drenched. Head to toe. From the depths of

her scalp, to the crusted innards of her socks. With what? *Oh.*

Her eyes have been closed this whole time. Curtains rise.

Her vision swims, at first. Fuck. A hand is reaching out to her,

from a pile of legs. They're covered in gashes, and dry, dark

muck.

She gags, and turns left. It's even worse. She's

surrounded by body parts. Mangled, piled like trash. She can't

scream. She fell into a secret mass grave, that forgot about the dirt. Now she's floating in a rigid, sticky pool. There's no *floor* below, or anything solid. Just death.

How deep does this pit go? Lazda fucked up. This is *exactly* what they wanted. She ran in here for a weapon, but now she can't find her footing. Flies are buzzing, above. She looks up. The ceiling is flat. A wooden plank is hanging over the pit, like a diving board.

It's only three feet above her head. Is it Dr. Irma's *observation deck*? What a hospital.

Something belches, below. A loud snap comes next. Body parts shift, all around. Then they start sinking. Shit. Quicksand is pulling Lazda down, and this pit could be *deep*. Fuck this.

She kicks, up and down. Her feet smash into *slush*. It makes a horrible suckling noise, like a horse clomping through mud. She reaches for the plank, grabs it, and pulls herself up. Air hisses, and lets go of her legs. She scrambles across the diving board, then bolts for the door.

Lazda shoves it open and leaps out of the cabin, like a fugitive from hell. She runs across the porch, dives off the steps, and collapses on the dirt below. She pants between birch stumps, while looking up at the stars. She'll spend her final moments outside, with the only friends she's ever known. It's nice, but she's waiting for Dr. Irma's machete to come down, like a guillotine.

Lazda hears a cough, instead. She gets up, and turns to the noise. Those static eyes are now standing by a tree. It's the last survivor, in this field of stumps. The birch is wearing a sign. Dr. Irma is holding her long blade up against its trunk, like the throat of a hostage. She asks.

"Did you like my hospital?"

Lazda shuts her eyes. She's back at that campfire with Oma. Her gaunt, wrinkled face is telling a story, but Lazda didn't hear it, when she was young. *Oh.* Dr. Irma cuts in.

"What did you yell earlier, about these trees? You said that they're *sacred,* didn't you?"

Lazda opens up, but still hears Oma's odd, gravelly whistling. Dr. Irma taps her blade on that lonely white trunk. The van's engine is rumbling, but the forest is quiet. Lazda says.

"They are."

And crosses her arms. Shadows grow longer, and taller, across the field of stumps. Irma and the pushers are twelve feet away. Have they noticed the silence? The men shuffle. Lazda looks down. Her poncho was silver, before the cabin. Now it's brown, red, purple, and black. Her hands are covered. So is her face. Her hair. She spits, but death won't leave her tongue.

Lazda should go jump into a stream, but something tells her: *be still*. That the way she is right now is the way to be. Why is instinct telling her to embrace this filth? Maybe it's *someone*.

Someone wrinkled, sitting by a campfire that burned out long ago.

"Your delusions are impressive, rabbit! I'm *fascinated*. Please, indulge me. If these trees are *sacred*, what will happen to me if I chop this one down?"

Birch trunks start getting whiter. Blades of grass and pebbles emerge, from shadows in the dirt. Dandelions whisper below. Lazda can see the whole forest now. Clouds must've moved away from the moon. Or, was it something else? Tension builds, in the field. The game's two minutes are long over, but no one seems to care. Lazda *could* run, but then she hears a noise.

It's melodic, in its own gravelly way. Her spine turns to ice. It's almost time. She asks.

"Can you hear them singing?"

Lazda can. Their whispered melody is almost like a lullaby. Dr. Irma frowns, and turns side to side. So do the bible pushers. Soon, they shrug and snicker. Sugar Boots yells.

"Hear *what*, you fucking bum!?"

Is he trying to get a promotion? Lazda quits being coy.

"*Oh*, Sugar Boots. You poor fool. You don't know about the guardians, do you?"

"What *guardians*?"

"They protect the forest. Trees turn black when they swoop in, to snatch wicked souls. They go to another realm. A place where time doesn't exist. Where minutes last for thousands of years. Evil tastes *delicious* to the guardians, and they savor every meal. No one knows how…"

"*ENOUGH*!!!"

Dr. Irma is shouting, but beneath her bluster, there's fear. The maniac keeps ranting.

"Tree spirits? Other realms? How do you come up with this shit? That was some *quality* improv, rabbit! But you guys believed her? Maybe *she* should come work for me instead!"

The pushers grumble. That whispered lullaby is getting louder. Dr. Irma goes on.

"But no, you're just a *BUM*. A superstitious waste of flesh, blood, and water. You still believe in fairy tales? Well, guess what? This is *my* land! And here, Santa Claus isn't real!"

THUNK. Dr. Irma jabs her machete into the trunk of her hostage. String snaps. The forest is still. Lazda shakes her head. *That* was a mistake. As the sign hits the dirt, Irma grunts. She tries to pull her machete out of the trunk, but her blade dug in deep. Leaves rustle. These trees are all connected. Wind howls, with a harsh, sulphury odor. The gravel lullaby is screaming, upstairs. It's time. Lazda smiles, like the witch in the woods that every kid was warned about.

"Still can't hear them singing? Here, let me help…"

Lazda starts whistling too. She's copying the melody that's looped in her head. Oma warned her. Only people like them can hear this music, but that by harmonizing *their* melodies, out loud, Lazda can help *expand their audience.*

Electricity is rushing through her. She's channeling a lot of

energy, and none of it belongs to her. It feels good. Too good.

"What the hell are you doing? Stop that!"

Lazda keeps whistling. Dr. Irma's breath starts smoking.

Sugar Boots and his Lap Dogs are rubbing their arms. It's getting

cold out here. The forest is starting to smell like a volcano.

The field of stumps darkens. It gets quiet. The van just

died.

Lazda walks away from the tombstones, and stops at the

edge of the cliff. She stares at all those bone-white spires. The

legion marches, all the way down. But then, at the bottom of the

mountain, the trees start vanishing. One by one at first, and then

in waves. Lazda asks.

"Can you hear them now?"

A dark avalanche is racing up the mountain. It's heading

right for them. Peebles vanish, with blades of grass. Evergreens

go dark. The cabin does too. Panic takes hold. Dr. Irma and the

bible pushers start running for the van, but it too gets swallowed

by the abyss. It's too late.

A black wave washes over them all. The guardians are here. They're angry, and hungry.

Dr. Irma screams. Lazda shuts her eyes. She hears thundering hooves. Hurricane winds smack into her, but she doesn't budge. Oma told her why. That campfire burned out long ago, but it's still warm. And death is saving Lazda. The old horse whisperer told her to cover herself in blood and rotten flesh, to seem *unappetizing* to the guardians. It must be working. Would this decay have stuck to her quite so well, without her tinfoil poncho? Maybe it *is* lucky.

Time crawls. Horrible screams and desperate pleas echo across the forest.

Ripples from the past wash over to the surface of this plain. Ancients torments still ongoing, and new nightmares that haven't begun.

Eventually, the wind slows. Screams fade. When the stink of sulfur is gone, Lazda opens her eyes. *Whoa.* There's still a field of stumps, but Dr. Irma and the pushers are gone. Even their footprints got swept away. She sees a big, empty crater, where the cabin once stood. The only trace of her captors that's left is the van. It's still parked, under legions of white spires.

Lazda thanks the trees for everything, but to Dr. Irma, and the others, these same birch trunks will soon resemble jail bars, with peeling paint. They were taken to another place, *far* worse than any hell they could've imagined. They mocked her legends, but Lazda knew the truth. *Never* disrespect a forest, especially at night.

Did she win their game? She never got a thousand bucks. Did Dr. Irma even have that cash? Probably not. Fuck it. Lazda looks ahead, to something even better. It might be fried, but it's a new place to sleep. She starts walking towards the van. *CRUNCH!*

Lazda looks down. She stepped on glowing glasses. Cracked honeycomb lenses flicker. She hears that orchestra of stacked voices. Dr. Irma's audience is screaming. All those people paid to watch Lazda die. What's happening to them? Maybe she expanded *their* audience, farther than she, or Oma, thought was possible. Will Lazda be the last thing they see?

She shrugs. In this awful, cleared out field, the last surviving birch is still standing.

It's time to heal. The van is open. Its keys are still in the ignition, and no one will claim this Black Maria anytime soon. Coyotes howl, close by. They tell Lazda to stay here for a while.

THE DAM

Jedd shoots the padlock. He hits *B*, and the gate swings open.

He steers the spy's hands. A short tunnel opens up to a beautiful panorama. They're on top of a dam. It's surrounded by mountains. There's a steep cliff on the left, and a big lake on the right. The water stretches out until it vanishes. Most ignore the scenery to focus on killing, but not Jedd. He studies the expanse. The secret island is out there. He just has to find it.

"What are you doing, Jedd? Jump off the cliff!"

Fucker. Brad just broke the illusion. Jedd sighs. He isn't a bad ass spy on a mission in a strange land. He's a kid, a kid that's sitting too close to a glowing TV. The rest of this bedroom is huge, and dark. But it isn't Jedd's room. This is Brad's house. They're having a sleepover.

Dogs bark outside. Crickets scream. It's late. They should be asleep, but duty calls. Jedd is comfy. This carpet is nice in here. It doesn't feel like a metal sponge. Brad is scowling next to Jedd on the floor, waiting for him to die. The brat wants the controller. Bad.

Officially, they're friends. Jedd and Brad are in the same fifth grade class. But they aren't in the same class, not really. Brad's bedroom is paradise. It's bigger than Jedd's house. It's full of toys. Posters of metal bands cover the walls. Kittie, Korn, Disturbed. Brad has his own TV, with the newest video game system, and the game that every kid wants to play. Brad is also an asshole, but here, Jedd feels free. Nothing reminds him of his mom in this room. At home, she's everywhere. She's been missing for years. Every time Jedd sees her things, darkness stabs his chest. It feels empty, infinite. He wonders if she's scolding him, or begging for help. *No thanks.*

Wind howls outside. Branches scratch the window. Brad shivers, but Jedd smiles. This big, dark room is full of dinosaurs, spacemen and soldiers. Nothing can hurt him in here. Brad is a jerk, but right now, Jedd has the controller. He stares at the world inside of the TV. He can do whatever he wants in there, except jump. He has three guns, and a license to kill. It's a nice place. Jedd doesn't want to leave. He wants to go deeper.

Maybe he can. He needs to find the secret island.

He read about it on *the internet*. The secret island is a strange, forbidden myth, hidden somewhere in this level. Officially, it's just a rumor. But Jedd was determined. It took an hour to load at the library, but he found a website, made by someone who actually got to the secret island. The webpage was a stark black screen. White letters spelled fifteen cryptic words.

Last dock. The only crate that explodes. Only the worthy will find the secret island.

"Quit *sightseeing,* Jedd! Start shooting! Hurry up! I wanna see the next level!"

Brad just wants an excuse to try and snatch the controller again, so Jedd says.

"Shut up, Brad. I'm looking for the secret island."

He steers the spy's hands past the ledge that ends this level. They go into a guard tower, down winding stairs, and out towards the concrete docks below, heading for the farthest one. The last dock. Jedd knows the way. Brad whispers.

"What secret island?"

The brat is curious, but he really wants blood, and the controller. Is he *worthy*? Jedd says.

"It's hidden in this level. I read about it at the library yesterday."

"What? A strategy guide came out for this game already?"

"No, Brad. I read about it on the internet."

"Yeah right, Jedd! Your family can't afford a computer!"

Brad laughs. Jedd wants to punch the brat. Hard, right in his spoiled mouth. He *definitely* isn't worthy. But Jedd has a mission, and this is Brad's house. Plus, his dad is terrifying. Jedd could easily hurt the brat, but he'll scream immediately, then Rick will come storming in here.

Jedd knows what to do. He'll steer the spy's hands in silence, until he calms down.

Yet by the time they make it all the way to the last dock, Jedd is even angrier. He hits *B*. Now the spy's hands have a sniper rifle. At the edge of the water, he holds down *R*.

Hands on the screen look into the scope, which zooms into the far side of the lake. Jedd exhales, gets lost in the snowy, pixelated mountains, and finally replies to the brat.

"You're right. They can't. But you didn't listen. *I said* that I read it at the *LIB-RAR-Y*!"

Brad waits, like he's expecting more, then shrugs.

"Whatever. *I* think that you're lying. You just wanna keep hogging the controller!"

Sheesh. What a greedy maniac. Jedd's had it for five minutes, tops. Dogs bark outside. Then a door slams, somewhere in this big house. Brad's eyes bulge with terror. He whispers.

"*Shh*! Be quiet! We're supposed to be asleep!"

Fuck off. Jedd keeps searching the lake through the sniper scope. He's used to Brad's bullshit. It's part of their routine. They hate each other. Jedd only hangs out with Brad for his TV. But why does the brat hang out with Jedd? What does Brad gain? It must be something, but what? His family has it all. In this house, Brad probably never hears about bills. He might not even know what they are. He's never felt their bite. When he hits a light switch, he never doubts if it'll work. Must be nice.

But *why* does Brad's family have it so easy? Is their life free of pain? Or do they suffer another way? Probably not. There's something deep, cruel and unfair about it all. But Jedd is too young to know what it is, or what to do about it, so he just comes over here to break Brad's toys, eat his food and act like an asshole. It's not even revenge. It's balance.

"So, where is this *secret island*?"

Brad's voice is shrill, even when he whispers. Jedd replies from the side of his mouth.

"I don't know, but I think it might be somewhere across the lake."

And keeps searching. He doesn't need to squint to look through the sniper scope, but he does anyway. It helps him forget that he's here, not there. He studies the lake and the mountains, one section at a time. These graphics are insane. They even have *fog* in this game! It all looks so real. How can graphics possibly get any better than this? Brad says.

"I can't see anything. These graphics suck. Maybe this *secret island* doesn't exist, Jedd."

His pudgy hand is squirming its way towards the controller. Jedd whispers.

"It has to! I saw it online! Why would someone make up a whole website, just to lie?"

Brad laughs. It's loud. Too loud. After the brat wheezes and catches his breath, he says.

"You're *so* gullible! You'll believe anything! Don't you remember what Dorothy said to everyone on the playground last year?"

Jedd narrows his eyes.

"No, Brad. I was sick that week, and no one was allowed to talk about it after."

"Oh. Well, *I* was there! It was nuts! Dorothy told us that Cecily's family were *cannibals*. She said she looked in their window, and saw them chopping up an arm! Right next to a boiling pot! We believed it. But later, we heard the truth. Dorothy made it all up. She saw it all in a movie. She lied, because she wanted to ruin Cecily's life."

Jedd shrugs and keeps scanning the lake with the sniper scope. He tuned out most of that. Brad loves the sound of his own voice.

The brat reads big books. He has a vocabulary. He thinks big words make him smart, but they just make him sound like an asshole who thinks he's better than everyone else. Fuck him. Why did Brad even bring Dorothy up? Are they still talking about the secret island?

Needles drill into Jedd's temples. He's sitting too close to the TV. The game's muzak whispers out of the glowing box. Brad coughs like he wants attention, or a reply. Jedd says.

"So?"

"People lie, Jedd. They do it all the time. Some, like Dorothy, get good at it. So good that they even start to believe their own lies."

"So?"

"*SO*?! Just because you saw something *online* doesn't make it true, Jedd! Of course they spent time on the website! Liars work too. Sometimes, they work harder than truth tellers."

Brad looks proud, like he just delivered a big, important speech. Jedd yawns.

"Whatever, Brad. I'm gonna keep..."

Something smashes into the wall. Tacks fall from posters. Jedd tenses up. Muffled voices start yelling from the other side of the wall. He can't hear what they're saying. It sounds like a man and a woman. Brad's parents? It's just them in this great big house, isn't it? Jedd whispers.

"What was that?"

Silence replies. Jedd looks at his friend. Brad's eyes went wide and vacant. The brat looks hypnotized. Is he?

Jedd should pinch his ear, or slap him. But then the muffled yelling fades. Brad blinks. His eyes lose their dull, static sheen. He went somewhere else, but now he's back. The brat looks around his dark, flickering room like he's seeing it all for the first time, then says.

"Tell me more about the secret island."

Brad is dodging the question, but Jedd won't spoil this sudden enthusiasm. He whispers.

"It was snuck into this level at the last minute, right before the game was released. Even the company who made it didn't know about the secret island."

Brad blinks. Greed returns to the brat's eyes, giving them life. He asks.

"What's there?"

"I don't know, but it must be something crazy. Top secret. I saw a website that was made by someone who actually got there. It said: *only the worthy will find the secret island.*"

"But *how* do we get there, Jedd?"

"I don't know. It didn't say. I guess we'll have to figure it out on our own."

Brad frowns like he smelled some shit. Jedd isn't surprised. He adds.

"But the website did have one more clue: *Last dock. The only crate that explodes.*"

"Are you serious, Jedd!? Really? *Every* fucking crate explodes in this game!"

Brad is right. Hell, even lamps explode. Bookshelves too. But not doors. Or walls. Safes and statues are immune as well. Is *that* what the clue is about? Brad asks.

"Well, what do *you* think is hidden on the secret island?"

His curiosity is burning. What indeed? Jedd keeps searching through the sniper scope. He heard creepy rumors about faceless soldiers, rooms that melt into the floor, and locked doors that shouldn't be opened. But he doesn't want to scare the brat. Yet. Jedd says.

"I don't know, Brad. It could be anything."

"*Whoa.* Maybe they'll let you play through the game as *Shark-Man!*"

Jedd blinks.

"Who?"

"You know, *Shark-Man*! The tall, scary guy from the spy movies, with the metal teeth."

Jedd laughs. He knows who Brad is talking about.

"His name isn't *Shark-Man,* you bonehead! It's *Jaws!*"

"*Jaws?*"

"Yeah, dude. *Jaws.*"

"That's stupid, Jedd."

"It might be a stupid name, but that's his name."

"I think you're wrong, puke-breath! It's *Shark-Man*!"

Brad's wrong, but without a third party to settle this argument, it'll never end. Jedd thinks of the slow-loading websites that he saw on the library computer. *The information superhighway*. Maybe, one day, the internet will be fast. Maybe it'll even fit in their pockets, like a calculator. Jedd smiles. When that day comes, it'll be *impossible* for guys like Brad to hide from the truth. Maybe the internet will make liars extinct, like the dinosaurs. That'd be nice, but that's not now.

Jedd gets an idea. He keeps pressure on the *R* button, but looks at Brad's bookshelf, scanning those VHS tapes for one featuring the man with metal teeth. Jedd looks behind all the jedis and soldiers sitting on the shelves, like construction workers eating lunch on a long steel beam.

He sees a dark pistol. A BB gun. It looks like the *PP7 Special Issue* in this game. Lucky bastard. Jedd's dad can't afford cool shit like this. Plus, he knows that his kids would just end up

245

using it to hurt each other. But Brad is an only child. His parents don't care who he shoots.

Jedd looks up at the next cube on the towering bookshelf, and feels a chill.

A shape that looks familiar is hiding up there, in the shadows.

Jedd squints. When his eyes adjust to the dark, he sucks in air through his teeth.

Five feathers and a thimble. Shit. It's the Black Ogre. The Kachina doll is hiding between figurines of Boba Fett and Darth Vader on top of the bookshelf, but Nata-Aska isn't a toy.

Jedd knows this spirit well. It's the worst possible one to find hiding in the dark. Nata-Aska has a long snout, and fangs. She has wide, deranged eyes. Big red ears. Five long feathers sprout from her black, thimble-shaped head. She's also holding a knife.

What is Nata-Aska doing up there? Why is she here?

Jedd feels darkness stab his chest. It's empty, infinite. Where is his mom? At this point, would it even be a good thing if she was still alive? Jedd keeps staring at Nata-Aska.

The Kachina doll is intricate, detailed, and hand-carved from cottonwood root. It wasn't cheap. Maybe Brad saw this icon in a fancy store, and threw a fit until it was his. It's his favorite cheat code in life, and money is no object to Brad's family. The brat probably picked out the Kachina with fangs and a knife because she *looked cool.* Does Brad think Nata-Aska is a toy? She's not. She's a bridge between realms, for the god that punishes children who misbehave.

Jedd gulps. Nata-Aska has two *very* promising subjects in this bedroom.

His mom was Hopi. She taught Jedd *all* about the Black Ogre. More like threatened. She told Jedd that if he was bad, one day, Nata-Aska would come visit him in the night. And if he couldn't account for his sins, or find a way to make them right, she'd snatch him up, and eat him.

Jedd turns back to the glowing TV. He can't think about Nata-Aska, or her fangs. He needs to find the secret island. Somewhere out there, a clock is ticking. He doesn't know when it'll chime, or what will happen when it does, but he knows it can't be much longer until it starts.

Goosebumps rise on the back of Jedd's neck. Shit. The Black Ogre is watching him.

Why did he even look at that damn bookshelf? Oh yeah. *Jaws*. Why bother? Even if Jedd had proof, Brad *still* wouldn't admit defeat. He'd dig in. The brat only sees what he wants to see.

"Oh! I got it, Jedd! *Now* I know why you think his name is *Jaws*!"

"Because that's his name?"

"No, because there's another movie called *Jaws*! But it's different. It's about sharks!"

Brad is hopeless.

Jedd gets lost in the scope, and his search. The lake is beautiful. This dam is in Russia. Jedd's dad said that country used to be scary, but now it's run by broke drunks. Do people say the same thing about Jedd's dad? What made Russia so scary? Will it ever be scary again?

The screen turns red.

The controller buzzes like an angry hornet.

A violent, crimson glow floods the bedroom. Clutter around Jedd grows ominous. Toys on the floor that looked fun earlier now look demonic, *alive*.

"*Shit*! Shoot them, Jedd!"

Brad isn't helping. The damage meter drops two bars. Jedd was too busy worrying about Nata-Aska. He forgot about the bad guys in this level who are trying to kill him. He snarls.

"What do you think I'm doing, Brad? Trying to make *friends*?"

Jedd hits *B*. When the spy's hands have a machine gun, they turn around.

A soldier in a green uniform snuck up behind them. This bad guy looks realistic, but he stands still and lowers his gun. It's as if he's begging Jedd to end it all. He *could* leave this pixelated being alone, but then the enemy soldier raises his rifle again. Too bad.

Jedd hits *Z*.

The spy's hands open fire. The enemy soldier falls to his knees and writhes on the ground, clutching at the new red splotch covering his neck. Brad exclaims.

"*WHOA*!! That was *awesome*!"

Of course. Add a little blood, and *now* the brat likes the graphics. Jedd whispers.

"Aren't we supposed to be quiet?"

The wall thuds, as if in reply. The impact is hard, like a bowling ball hit it from the other side. Powder rains from the ceiling. Tacks fall from posters, vanishing into the carpet below. Now they'll wait like landmines, for unsuspecting feet. Jedd freezes in place, just like he did when he walked in front of an angry rattlesnake on a trail. He won't even move the spy's hands.

Something big and heavy falls in the next room. It makes the floor rattle. Was it hanging from the wall? Not anymore. Fallout spreads. The last tack falls from the Kittie poster, and it drops next. The four ladies glide down slow, like it's an elevator. The shouting resumes. It got louder. Maybe the thing that fell was muffling noise. Now Jedd hears what they're saying.

"Don't you fucking *dare* tell me how to…"

"It's just a game, Rick!"

"*Just* a game!?! Listen to yourself, Doris! Him and that little shithead friend..."

"*Rick*! He's just a little boy! Jedd is sweet..."

"Sweet? He's nothing but trouble! I knew it from the first time *our* son..."

Brad is dreaming with his eyes open again. He's in another place. He must visit often. Jedd sees a pattern. To Brad, shouting and thuds are just another unpleasant part of the house that no one talks about, like a dark stain in the bathroom, or a door that he isn't supposed to open.

Another thud hits, but this one is soft. At least, softer than the others. The wall doesn't rattle this time. Other posters stay put. Korn and Limp Bizkit are safe, but Kittie fell behind the bed. Yet their poster landed upright. It's wedged behind the bed. The lady's eyes are peeking out from behind Brad's pillow. Jedd has a crush on Fallon, the guitarist with red hair. He smiles at her, then remembers all the times that Brad bragged about his dad's gun collection.

Rick is terrifying. He has hot breath and mean eyes, on a good day. And tonight, judging from what Jedd has heard so far, he's in rare form.

Rick knows that Jedd and Brad are awake, breaking rules. *His* rules. Does he *teach* Brad *lessons* too? Probably.

The TV flashes red, again.

Jedd turns the spy's hands and hits *Z*. The controller buzzes. A new bad guy flails like a ragdoll and vanishes. Brad whispers.

"You're getting sloppy! Now you only have one health bar left!"

Jedd seethes. Now he knows why his dad hates back seat drivers. But his dad hates a lot of things. It makes sense. He's angry. So is Jedd. They've both been that way, ever since his mom disappeared. It's been years, and he still doesn't know what happened to her. Apparently, Hopi women like his mom go missing all the time in America. At first, Jedd had hope. He saw a lot of action movies that started when people went missing. He thought it was a big deal. He thought people would care about his missing mother. He was wrong.

No one cared. No one wanted to talk about it either.

It's been years, but it still hurts, every single day. Part of him still thinks that somewhere out there, his mom is still alive. Waiting to be rescued. Waiting for people who aren't looking. It's agony. No wonder he's angry.

Jedd and his dad did everything, that they could afford. They even tried to raise money to hire a private detective, but their *neighbors* only coughed up five bucks.

Jedd shakes his head. He's getting distracted. Brad almost snatched the controller.

Jedd hits *pause* to check on his health bar. Shit. One more shot will be fatal. Sweat drips down his forehead. It feels like he's in the game. If the spy's hands die, will Jedd? No, he'll just have to give the controller to Brad. It's the sacred code between all gamers who only have one.

The brat is smiling. He saw the same health bar. Shit. Jedd has to find the secret island. If Brad takes control of the spy's hands, the search will be over. At least the wall hasn't thudded for a couple minutes. But Rick could still burst in here, any second. Jedd needs to concentrate. Brad yawns. Loud, like a spoiled cub. He groans.

"You're almost dead. We're *never* going to find this island, Jedd. I'm getting tired…"

"Go to sleep then!"

"But I can't go to sleep, Jedd. Not until you do."

What? Jedd hits *start*. As the spy's hands check their watch, he turns to Brad and asks.

"What the fuck are you talking about? Why not?"

The brat says nothing. It makes his answer even creepier.

The quiet drags on while the game's pause muzak plays softly from the glowing TV. Does the brat think his toys will get stolen? Maybe he wants to fuck with Jedd. Brad replies.

"Because that's what Taylor told me."

Ice creeps down Jedd's spine. He thinks about the BB gun and asks.

"Who's Taylor?"

Brad points at his bookcase. It's the shelf that Jedd was trying to avoid. He sees Nata-Aska. Her long snout. Her fangs. Her five long feathers, her big red ears. One hand is holding a

knife. The other has a bundle of arrows. Her blade gleams from
the TV's glow, like a real knife. But it isn't real. Is it? Where's
her bow?

And why does Brad think Nata-Aska's name is *Taylor*?

Jedd turns away from the Black Ogre. It doesn't get
better. Brad's eyes have a new, excited glaze. Simplistic,
determined. The glare of a fanatic. Maybe he *does* know about
the powers of the Kachina doll that's hiding up there, between
Boba Fett and Darth Vader.

Jedd shivers. This is bad. Real bad. He whispers, with a
faint trace of hope.

"Your *doll* said that you can't go to sleep, until I do?"

Jedd prays that Brad will call him crazy.

"He's not a doll, Jedd. His name is Taylor. And yes, he
did."

The brat shrugs, like he said something that's obvious,
even normal. Then he asks.

"Are you *sure* the secret island is real?"

Jedd should find out what Brad knows about Nata-Aska,
but he looks at the glowing TV instead. He should uncover the

Black Ogre's plans, and figure out how to stay awake all night, but he hits *start* and gets lost in the little details of the dam, the mountain and the lake.

The spy's hands are on the edge of a concrete dock. It juts out into the lake that the dam created. The platform is sparsely decorated. Wood crates, metal crates, oil barrels. What fun. It's all useless. The clock is ticking. How long until Brad gets bored and flips out? Who cares?

Jedd pretends the spy's hands are his own. He can almost feel the cold breeze blowing in from the lake, and smell the fresh, salty air. He thinks about the clue from that website at the library.

Last dock. The only crate that explodes.

Why not? Jedd hits *Z*. Predictable flames burst from a wood crate. Shit. What now? Who cares? Maybe *not* finding the secret island is the key. Jedd holds *R* and watches the spy's hands look through the scope. It's nice here. There's no shitty friends, screaming parents, or Nata-Aska in this world. But Jedd doesn't live in the glowing TV. Brad shouts.

"What's that!?!"

Shit. That was *way* too loud. Brad crossed the line, but he's pointing at the glowing TV.

Jedd sees another concrete platform in the scope. A dock, on the other side of the lake.

Holy shit. It's the secret island.

The myth is tiny and blurry in the scope, but it's there. Jedd studies every pixel. There are two structures on the concrete platform. A tall guard tower and an armored hut with a gatling gun sticking out. A gate stands between them. It looks like the sliding metal door leads into the mountain itself. The secret island is like a hinge, a hidden bridge between them. Jedd exclaims.

"We found the secret island!"

His imagination is running wild. What could be hiding over there?

Like any good secret, this one just revealed more mysteries. Are there new weapons over there? What's behind the sliding gate? Does it open up to an entire new game, hidden within this game? Anything seems possible. Brad rubs his hands together and says.

"So, how do we get there?"

"I don't know."

Jedd shrugs and keeps staring at the glowing TV. Brad punches the floor and yells.

"What do you mean, Jedd? *You said* that you knew how to get there! You *lied* to me!"

The brat's eyes are shaking in their sockets, but anger is contagious. Jedd shouts.

"You're losing it, Brad! I didn't lie about shit! I *never* said that I knew how to get there!"

And panics. That was *way* too loud. But whatever. Brad went too far first. Earlier, he said that *liars work harder than truth tellers*. He's proving it now. Brad says.

"Are you telling me that we have to figure it out on our own?"

"*Yes,* Brad! That's the point! We're friends, and friends solve mysteries together!"

"You think we're *friends,* Jedd?"

Brad laughs. His eyes darken at the same time. Now they look grizzled, old. Cold breath whistles behind Jedd's neck.

Maybe his fears were misplaced. Maybe Rick and Nata-Aska aren't the real monsters in this house. Maybe it's Brad. The brat keeps talking.

"I know what you're up to. My daddy told me. He said that *poor* people like you *leech*. Do you know what leeches are? They latch onto your flesh, to suck your blood. They won't let go until you *burn* them off. And that's what my daddy said you are, Jedd. A leech, on me. You break my toys and hog my TV. All you do is take. And lie. Enough, Jedd. You don't like me, and I don't like you, so let's stop pretending."

It's almost hilarious. Jedd is caught in a trap. He should punch Brad, but he can't, because the brat will summon his psychotic father. But if Jedd talks, he'll get mad enough to lash out. He sees empty Surge cans on the floor. Greasy paper plates with abandoned pizza crusts, like tombstones. He doesn't get *any* of this shit at home. But he doesn't blame his father.

"*Wow*, Jedd. You *really* have nothing to say for yourself, huh? I must've hit a nerve."

Jedd exhales slow. *Now* he knows what to say to the brat.

"If you *really* think that I just use you for your stuff, then why do you hang out with me?"

"You wanna know? Ok, Jedd. Why not? You see, my daddy told me something else about leeches like you. He said that I can leech from you too."

Wind howls outside. What happened to the dogs? Something with claws is scratching on the window. He looks up. It's a thorn tree. Jagged branches with fangs are blocking the window and casting strange shadows. A new beam emerges from this funnel, shining like a spotlight. Where's it pointing? Jedd follows its trail, until he sees where it's going. Shit. No way. He won't look up there, but he feels that glare. Nata-Aska is watching him. *Here we go again.*

Jedd can't get away from his mother. She's missing, but she's everywhere.

The stab hits his chest, but this time, it isn't darkness. At least, not all of it. There are hints of light, even song. Being reminded of his mom will always be painful, but sometimes, it'll also be beautiful. Like it is now. Jedd realizes that she hasn't been begging for help all these years, or scolding him. She's been watching Jedd. Protecting him. Knowing this, something different burns in his chest. It hasn't been there for a long time. Warmth. Yet Brad keeps talking.

"That's right, Jedd! My daddy says that you have to fight for the things that *I take for granted*. He says that you have *street smarts,* and that I need them. So I do what you do. I take. You get it yet? You leech from me, and I leech from you, but we aren't friends."

Jedd smiles. He'll teach Brad all about *street smarts*. The first class will be about phone books, bars of soap in socks, and how to hurt someone without making a mark. Jedd says.

"I see, Brad. You don't want to find the secret island together. You just want *me* to find it, *for* you. And if I can't do things *for* you, then I'm worthless *to* you. Is that right?"

"*Exactly,* Jedd! And if you can't get to the secret island, give me the fucking controller!"

Brad lunges at Jedd. He wants to hit the brat, but he won't. Not in front of Nata-Aska.

A strange sort of wrestling match begins.

They're hitting all the buttons on the controller while fighting for it. What are they making the spy's hands do? Brad pulls hair and throws clumsy, pillow-like punches. Jedd sees many soft spots on the brat that he could jab, but he just tries to hold onto the controller. Then he sees the poster that fell behind the bed. Jedd looks at Fallon's eyes as he pushes back with kid gloves. She comforts him, but it's not enough. Jedd is about to lose control.

Gunfire erupts from the glowing TV.

Shit. Another ambush? Jedd looks up.

No, their fight is just making the spy's hands shoot at a metal crate.

At first, Jedd shrugs. Then the metal crate explodes.

Brad stops struggling. Jedd blinks. What the fuck? Metal crates don't explode in this game. They never have, until now. Why? Was that specific crate special? Or is it the last dock?

Oh.

They must be close. Then Brad lunges for the system itself, shouting.

"*FINE.* If you won't give up the controller, then *maybe* we should just…"

Brad grabs the cartridge. Shit. He's going to yank it out of the system, while it's still on. Fuck this. Jedd gets up and throws the brat away from his own game system.

Brad hits the floor like a bag of bowling balls. The TV flickers. Oh no. Was he too late? Jedd looks down. A corner of the cartridge is loose, but the rest of it is still in the system and holding on. What will happen now? Is Brad going to scream? The brat looks up and says.

"*Whoa.*"

Jedd drops the controller.

The spy's hands are walking on water.

What the fuck? Somehow, by fighting over the controller, they accidentally hit the *exact* right combination of buttons, in *just* the right place. And when the game cartridge was partially removed from the system, it all came together.

Now the spy's hands are gliding across the lake, and heading for the secret island. How? Did they summon some kind of invisible boat? Jedd isn't controlling the game. No one is. The spy's hands are moving on their own now. The secret island is getting closer.

The snowy mountains are growing. So is the forbidden concrete dock.

Jedd gets up and turns up the TV. It's a risky move, but they just unlocked a legendary secret. He has to hear what happens next. But it's quiet. The game's background muzak is gone.

Something crashes into the wall instead. That one was *loud*. It left a mark.

"Stop it, Rick! *DON'T*..."

The wall thuds again. Cracks form, but Jedd doesn't care. Then Brad says.

"We did it, Jedd! We're going to the secret island!"

Jedd ignores the brat that he'll never forgive. He twists the volume knob all the way up, but still hears nothing. The secret island is growing. The spy's hands are halfway to the other side of the lake. The dock, the guard tower, the snowy mountain and the gate are all enlarging, revealing new shades of grey, black, brown and blue.

That gatling gun torrent is getting closer as well. The drone gun seemed harmless from afar, but now Jedd sees dark lines of detail in the long barrel. Is it going to open fire when they get close? Maybe it was put there to keep lucky intruders away. Shit.

Jedd only has one life bar left. Dying now is unthinkable. They're so close.

A crash makes him jump. The loudest one yet. The bedroom gets bright. Jedd looks up. There's now a big shadow being cast on the wall above the TV. It's shaped like a man. Jedd doesn't want to look away from the wonders on the screen, but he can't help it. He turns around.

A portal opened up at the other end of the room. The lights from the hallway are blaring.

A big man is swaying in the doorway. It's Brad's father.

Rick is wearing a dirty bathrobe and untied boots. He's holding a bottle with one hand, and hiding something behind his back with the other. Rick leans against the door that he just kicked down. His stained undershirt is on backwards, but Rick is alert, *wide* awake. Hatred is burning in his cloudy, bloodshot eyes. He points at Jedd and yells.

"*I KNEW* THAT YOU WERE A..."

Rick interrupts himself with a long, drawn-out belch.

It's almost musical, and reeks like the stinging stuff that doctors pour on cuts, even from here. Rick wipes his mouth, takes long, big glugs from his whiskey bottle, then says.

"Do you know what the *castle doctrine* is, boy?"

Jedd gulps. He says nothing, and turns to Brad. The brat is still staring at the TV. His eyes are glazed. After his dad kicked down his door, he must've went back to the other place. Jedd knows the feeling. He wants to witness the mythical secret that they unlocked too. He almost turns back to the TV, but then Rick shows Jedd what he was hiding behind his back.

It's a revolver. The gun looks like the cougar magnum from this game, but the real life version is more rusty than silver. It seems larger up close, and far more terrifying. Rick says.

"No? It's a law. It says that if *my* family is in danger, on *my* property..."

He looks past Jedd and stares at the TV. A flash of recognition makes Rick grin.

"...Then I have a license to kill. You attacked my son. Broke his arm. Almost strangled him too, but luckily, I got here in time, and did what I had to do, to protect Brad. You get it yet? I can kill you right here, right now, and never serve time. Your dad can't afford *a* lawyer, let alone the *lawyers* it'll take to fight me. After we're done, I'll call the sheriff myself. When he arrives with a body bag and a six pack, we'll drink and shoot the shit, while he does the paperwork."

Rick aims the six shooter at Jedd and clicks the hammer back.

"You see, hillbilly, it pays to have friends in high places."

It sounded like a snapping bone. Jedd gulps. He knows how Brad will get the injuries that'll be blamed on him. Shit. Really? Jedd doesn't want to die. Not now. He hasn't even gotten laid yet. He hasn't even *wanted* to. But what can he do? Fuck it.

Jedd turns away from the drunk *grown-up* that's pointing a gun at him and stares back at the glowing TV.

The secret island is close.

The mountain is enormous. The hidden dock is much larger than it looked in the scope, but the spy's hands are still gliding across the lake. The drone gun is getting closer too. The gatling gun's barrel starts turning. Oh fuck.

"*Goddamnit,* boy! *Look at me* when I'm talking to you!"

Damn. Jedd almost forgot about Rick. But he won't look away from the TV, or let go of the controller either, even though the spy's hands have gone rogue. Fuck it. Jedd didn't live long, but if he goes down in history as the kid who found the secret island, he'll be ok with that on his tombstone. Maybe they'll bury his mom next to him, if they ever find her.

Then something falls behind him. The crash is loud. It sounded heavy.

It came from the bookshelf. What fell? Jedd hopes it was the gun, and not Nata-Aska. But then he remembers his mom. This time, there's barely any pain in his chest. He just gets an idea. Maybe Nata-Aska would be a good thing. She's a god who punishes shitty kids, and there's a wide selection to choose from in here. Drunk *adults* act like kids too. The worst kind. Mean, stupid, prone to fits of madness. And Rick is acting like a *real* bad kid. A big, dangerous brat with a gun, who thinks he's a grown-up.

But Jedd won't look away from the TV. Footsteps thud behind him.

"Rick!?! What the fuck are you doing?!?"

It must be Doris. Brad's mom just walked into quite a mess. She yells.

"PUT THAT DOWN! *NOW*!"

Jedd hears smacks, cracks and thudding footfalls behind him, but he won't look away from the TV. The spy's hands are almost there. Brad is still sitting next to him on the floor. The brat is still transfixed by the glowing screen, even though his parents are fighting for a gun.

Jedd doesn't blame him. A thud shakes the floor. It sounded like a body. Who fell?

Doris groans. Shit. Rick snorts in triumph, takes a step forward, then hisses in pain.

"*AH*!!! BRAD!!! I just stepped on a *goddamn* tack!"

Jedd and Brad say nothing. The TV is still silent. The secret island is close, but not close enough. The spy's hands still need a minute to get there. It's a long trip across the lake.

"*BRAD*!!! *Are you even listening to me*!?! *I TOLD YOU* to clean your fucking room!!!"

The wind dies down outside. The claws are gone. The dog stopped barking long ago. Then Doris starts cackling from the floor. She's cracking up. Laughter is normally contagious, but not now. Her voice sounds different. It's smoky, wheezy, somehow more hollow.

Jedd stays focused on the TV. The shoreline is close. The gatling gun hasn't opened fire yet, but maybe it's waiting until he takes his first step on the forbidden dock. Or maybe the real gun behind him will start blasting first. Rick shouts.

"God-*DAMMIT* Brad! Look away from that damn TV for…"

A throat clears, loud enough to interrupt him. Who the hell was that? It didn't sound like Brad's mom, but it was. When Doris speaks, she has a new voice.

"Oh, *Rick*. Look at you. You might just be the worst kid that I've ever met."

It sounds hollow, gravelly. Jedd hears shuffling clothing next. Doris must be getting up. What now? He's *almost* there. He's ten seconds away from the secret island. Maybe less. Jedd doesn't want to look away now, but he has to know. He turns around, one last time.

Shit. Nata-Aska is standing upright on the carpet. Somehow, the Kachina doll *fell* off the bookcase. Now Nata-Aska is next to Doris, who's standing between Jedd and Rick's gun. Brad's mom has her back turned to Jedd. She's protecting him. Why? Jedd can't see Doris's face, but Rick can. His eyes are bulging. His mouth is hanging open. He's horrified. Why?

Jedd looks at the Kachina doll. Something is missing. Her knife is gone.

Doris is holding a knife instead. The blade is huge. Where did it come from? The bruised woman in the white nightgown didn't walk in here with a knife. Did she? Rick says.

"Honey?"

Doris chuckles with a throat full of gravel. Rick gulps, and Jedd turns to the glowing TV.

His timing is perfect. Holy shit. They did it. The spy's hands crossed the lake.

They're standing on the secret island.

A rush of euphoria floods Jedd's brain. He found it. He's *worthy*.

The spy's hands are still. Jedd moves the joystick, and they comply. He's back in control. He wants to explore. He wants to see it all. What's in the guard tower? Can he get inside the tall metal shell that houses the drone gun? Maybe not. That gatling gun barrel is still spinning.

Jedd wants to look at the dam from the other side of the lake. He wants to run around in circles, throw down the controller, shriek, and take pictures of the TV with a disposable camera, to immortalize his triumph.

But Jedd doesn't have time to do all those things. He can only pick one, and he has to see what's behind the gate. The one that leads into the mountain. Rick asks.

"*Doris*? What's wrong with your…"

Footsteps dart forward. Doris must be running.

Jedd steers the spy's hands towards the gate, and hears a metal click. Rick just pulled the trigger, but there's no explosion. A new noise is playing from the TV instead.

It's a cougar magnum. The revolver in the game just fired off a shot.

What the fuck? Rick screams. Jedd hears wet, slashing noises behind him. Chomping as well. He thinks about the doll's long snout, and knows what was wrong with Doris. Her teeth.

But Jedd doesn't look away from the screen. The spy's hands are in front of the gate.

This is it. Jedd just has to hit *B*, and he'll find out what's back there.

The screen flickers before he can. Sparks fly from the video game system below.

Shit. No. Not now. They're popping out from the crevice between the system and the exposed part of the cartridge. Jedd keeps his finger over the button. Will he electrocute himself if he presses it? The chomping and chewing noises stop. All he hears is dripping. Rick isn't yelling anymore. Then Brad shakes his head and groans, like he just woke up. The illusion has been broken for the brat. As if someone pulled him out of it. Someone who thinks he isn't *worthy*.

Brad rubs his eyes. When he looks away from the TV, his eyes pop.

Jedd doesn't need to turn around to know why. Anything his ears missed can be seen in Brad's face. It's the expression of a soft jelly donut that just woke up in a warzone. Brad shouts.

"*MOM?!?!*"

He's terrified, of her. Rick stopped squeezing the trigger, or doing anything else, but the phantom magnum is still blasting in the TV. Doris coughs, and groans like she just woke up too. She murmurs, touches something, and screams. Brad joins in. They almost harmonize.

Jedd sees a moving shadow from the corner of his eye, with feathers, fangs and paint. It's Nata-Aska, the Black Ogre. She's close. Jedd has to focus. The spy's hands are still in front of the gate. All he has to do is hit a button.

"What have I done?!??"

Doris is terrified, whimpering. Her nightgown probably isn't white anymore. Brad wails too, like a racecar engine that's deep in the red. His mom doesn't know what to do, or even what happened. Fuck. But Jedd gets an idea. A good one. The best he's ever had. It all comes together in an instant. Total and complete, damn near gift-wrapped. Jedd says.

"Castle Doctrine."

And hits *B*.

Sparks stop flying out of the system. The gate is opening.

The TV starts whistling like a boiling kettle. Jedd is transfixed. He can't look away. White light is shining behind the sliding metal gate. It's piercing, like staring directly at the sun.

But Jedd doesn't shield his eyes from the glare. Why would he?

The whistling tea kettle is getting louder. The spotlight gets brighter.

Jedd isn't alarmed. Somehow, he knows. This is how it has to be. The whole room turns white. He can't see his arms anymore. Or his legs. All he sees is white. Whistling gets louder.

It smothers the screams. Everything is white. And warm. Jedd shuts his eyes and surrenders.

Then screams.

Jedd blinks and rubs his eyes. A cool breeze blows across the lake. It smells like salt and incense.

The gate shuts behind him. The guard tower next to him is empty, just like his source said it would be. Jedd has a mission, and the clock is ticking. This one is personal. He's here to take back a sacred artifact. It once belonged to his mother. She might even be here as well.

It's time to move. The dam is on the other side of the lake.

BIRD
DANIELS

"Hey! Aren't you that Bird Daniels guy?"

Bird sighs. The sweaty man standing over his seat has excited, pig-like eyes. He's bald, with cargo shorts and a Hawaiian shirt. It's hot in this plane. The air is stale. People are tense and whispering. Bird was already having a bad day, then this plane got hijacked. He says.

"Yes, but right now, I'm not what you should be…"

"I knew it!"

Sweaty turns around and shouts to the rest of the passengers in the cabin.

"Hey, everyone! It's okay! Relax! This isn't a real hijacking at all! It's a prank! *Bird Daniels* is here! We're all going to be on TV!"

Joy washes over the passenger's faces. They light up with the delicate, giddy joy that people experience when they get close to fame of any kind. Applause erupts. Men comb their hair, women check their pocket mirrors, but no one looks around for the camera crew. There isn't one of course, but they don't care.

They want to believe. They're still clapping. Some rise for a standing ovation. Everyone is happy, except for three stewardesses and the three stocky women holding homemade shivs to their throats.

The hijackers are wearing red berets and cheap, tropical tourist outfits. The swim shorts, sandals and oversized floral shirts are their disguise. The women put on their berets as they pulled out their sharpened toothbrushes and started barking orders. The stewardesses still look terrified, but now the passengers think it's all part of the gag. Bird wants to help the women in humiliating uniforms, but how? He stares at the cup of melted ice in front of him, and all the empty mini bottles around it. It's a bad time to be hammered.

Bird was already hopeless before he got on board. He hated being defined by his prank TV show, but then his producer fired him this morning. Now he's getting replaced by someone younger. It figures. The show consumed Bird. He never landed any other roles. His unfinished script is an industry joke. But now he lost the show too. When the checks dry up, so will his lavish lifestyle. Bird thought being broke and forgotten was the worst thing that could happen, but now he's drunk, in a dire situation, and everyone thinks it's a prank. *His* prank, for a show that's no longer his.

The hijackers are confused. They don't know why their hostages are so happy. They're losing control. There are fifty passengers in the cabin, and three of them. Prison toothbrushes won't do much against a pig pile. The fourth hijacker is in the cockpit. A loudspeaker chirps.

"Ladies and, gentlemen...hello! This is your, captain speaking. Our flight will be making a slight detour. We apologize for any delays. Please, just be calm, and..."

A muffled voice whispers in the background. The captive pilot's voice grows serious.

"...Just do whatever the fuck they tell you to do. *Please!*"

Sweaty belches. He's still standing over Bird's seat. Sweaty looks around and says.

"Damn, Bird! You got the captain in on it too, huh?"

The passengers laugh throughout the cabin. This is bad. The hijackers dart their heads around. They're angry, and scared.

They think a hostage uprising is growing. Maybe they're starting to realize that threatening the life of someone in the service industry isn't exactly a great way to make a plane full of Americans follow orders.

What can Bird do? Passengers start rising from their seats, like the plane parked at the gate. The hijackers tense up, but the people swarm past them. They don't notice, or care, that the hijackers are still in *character*. They're ignoring inconvenient sights to keep their happy narrative safe. They head to the back of the plane and start raiding the booze cabinets.

Sweaty is still hovering over Bird's seat. He smells like fast food and looks proud of himself. He started this uprising. No one is questioning if Sweaty is wrong. They want to believe him. Partying is easier than facing reality. Bird was doing the same thing, before the women with red berets stood up and started shouting.

Now everyone is roaming the aisles, chugging looted booze and shouting. Someone starts playing Chumbawumba on their phone. A party rages all around the hijackers. No one is paying attention to them anymore. A squat woman with leathery skin and an eyepatch presses her sharpened toothbrush closer to the stewardesses neck and yells, but no one can hear her over the racket, not even Bird. No one cares. He has to do something. Bird stands on his seat, hits his head on the ceiling, waves to the whole cabin and shouts as loud as he can.

"Hey! Listen to me! This is a *real* hijacking! This isn't a prank! Those women are going to *kill* the stewardesses! Get back in your seats and calm the fuck down!"

The passengers laugh. Sweaty shouts.

"Sure, buddy! I bet that's what you *always* say, right before the cameras are revealed! Nice try, but you're not fooling *us*! Not today!"

Fuck. Bird tries to think, but his wet brain won't let him. He has to convince these idiots that he isn't lying to them, but he's a professional liar. He's going to watch these women die, and when Sweaty and the other passengers finally see what Bird is trying to tell them, they're going to blame *him* for it all! Bird knows it. *Fuck him! Do you know how rich he is?* On and on it goes.

There's only one thing Bird can do. He has to talk to the hijackers. He hopes they don't kidnap famous people. Bird gets down from his seat, shoves Sweaty out of the way and walks up to the woman with an eyepatch. The stewardess in her grip isn't scared anymore. She's furious. No one gives a shit if she dies, and she noticed. Bird puts his hands up and says.

"Hello, Ma'am. My name is Bird Daniels, and we need to talk."

The woman with an eyepatch frowns and says.

"Hello, shithead. My name is Rosa, and who the fuck do you think you are?"

Bird smirks and says.

"I'm the guy who can tell you why your hostages stopped listening to you."

"Oh, really? And why is that, Mr. *Bird*?"

"They think you and your friends are part of my TV show."

"What TV show?"

It's been a long time since Bird met someone who hasn't heard of his show. He always craved this moment of anonymity, but it couldn't be happening at a worse time. Bird says.

"We do pranks on people. We scare them with elaborate set-ups like this, and film it all."

"So you lie to people, and scare them, to entertain others?"

"I know, I know. I'm a real piece of shit. But all these people watch my show, and now they think they're part of it."

Rosa shakes her head like she's trying to wake up from a bad dream and says.

"They think they're on TV? Right now?"

"You guessed it. They think this is a joke."

Rosa snarls and says.

"I'll show them a *joke.*"

The stewardess tenses up. The fear has returned. Bird looks at her and says.

"What's your name?"

The stewardess croaks.

"Libra."

Bird smiles at Libra. Rosa scowls. She didn't want to know her name. Bird says.

"Killing Libra won't work. They'll think the blood is fake. They'll clap. They'll cheer."

Rosa looks shocked. Apparently, where she's from, people care about the lives of people in the service industry. It must be a strange place. Rosa says.

"So, these Americans don't care if I kill her, and watch shows full of lies?"

Bird shrugs and says.

"Land of the Free, Home of the Brave."

Rosa frowns, but lets the stewardess go. Libra hugs Bird, then glares at the passengers in the cabin with rage and utter disgust. She hates them more than the woman who almost cut her throat. At least Rosa cared if Libra lived or died. Bird asks.

"What is this all about anyway? Why did you hijack this plane?"

Determined idealism starts radiating from Rosa's bloodshot eye. She says.

"We just want to get back to our country, our people. A revolution just toppled our dictator, but he was your president's friend. So America hates our revolution, and made our island a no-fly zone. Many of us fled abroad to escape our dictator's secret prisons. Now we want to return. But American fighter jets will shoot down any plane that tries to land on our island. But they won't shoot down a plane full of American hostages, will they?"

Rosa is proud of her plan, and their revolution. Bird is starting to like her. He asks.

"What are you going to do with us after you land?"

Rosa looks confused, then she gets angry. She almost shouts, but whispers instead.

"We're going to let you go…What do you think we are, Mr. Bird? Animals? Butchers?"

Bird smirks. The devil on his shoulder is giving him a lot of ideas. He says.

"The thought never crossed my mind. But I'm not sure if that's such a good idea."

"What do you mean?"

"Don't get me wrong, your plan is brilliant. But the ending needs work. If you're worried about fighter jets, well, they won't bomb your island if it's full of American hostages either."

Rosa smiles like she just met her new best friend. She pats Bird's shoulder and says.

"You're a leader, Mr. Bird. Good in front of the camera. We need someone like you in our revolution. Our island is beautiful. Tell me, do you hate your life in America?"

Bird opens up his heart and speaks the truth.

"Every single day, Rosa."

She nods. So do the other women with red berets. They let the stewardesses go. Instead of running to the other passengers, the women in humiliating uniforms stay put. Rosa says.

"That's good, Mr. Bird. Do you want to join our revolution?"

"Yes."

Maybe getting fired is the best thing that ever happened to Bird Daniels. This could be a fresh start. Rosa respects Bird for what he *could* be, not what he's known for. She says.

"That's good. Very good. Now tell me, how the hell do I get these pigs under control?"

Bird smiles. He's the son of pig farmers from Georgia. He knows how to get pigs under control. He turns to the cabin. Some passengers sat down. Some are still prowling the aisles. Their faces are flushed. The altitude and the raided liquor is hitting them hard. The Macarena is playing now. The youngest hijacker is tapping her foot. She's never heard the song before. Her older friends shoot her death stares until she's still again. Bird takes a bow and shouts.

"Thank you! Thank you!"

The music stops. The passengers clap. They're ready for a pleasing voice to tell them what they want to hear. Bird says.

"My sweaty friend over there was right, this is all part of my show!"

The passengers go nuts. Bird senses anger rising from Rosa, but he keeps talking.

"My producers are upset with me. They don't want me to jump the gun on this, but I can't wait any longer! I just *have* to share this exciting news with all of you!"

Sweaty shoves other reveling passengers aside and shouts.

"What news?!?"

Sweaty doesn't like losing the spotlight. He isn't humbled by his fifteen seconds of fame, he thinks he deserves more. He'll learn to be careful what he wishes for. Bird says.

"This isn't a normal episode of my show."

A hush descends over the crowd. Bird points at Sweaty and says.

"When you, yes *you*, spoiled the prank earlier, I knew this crowd was too smart for my show's usual format. So tonight, we're doing something brand new, *just because of you*!"

Smiles fade. The crowd starts getting nervous, and angry. They're looking at Sweaty. His pig eyes are shifting around. He's starting to learn that attention isn't always a good thing. Someone shouts.

"What is it? What's the new twist?"

Bird smirks. He's going to enjoy this more than anything he's enjoyed in years. He's crossing the Rubicon. There's no turning back, and Bird is thrilled. He says.

"This prank never ends."

THE WALK-IN

Lydia leaves the walk-in fridge grinning. That felt good. She screamed in that cold metal box for thirty whole seconds, a lifetime during a rush. It was euphoric, even though it smelled like rotten dairy in there. She made friends with old chunks of food hiding on the floor, and a strange cake surrounded by plastic sheets and metal shelves. Lydia hopes no one is going to eat it, but then remembers why she had to go scream in a fridge, and hopes everyone gets seconds.

The rest of this kitchen looks even worse than the walk-in. Buzzing fluorescent lights above are even more soul crushing than the kind they have at the DMV. The walls are grey. So are the floors. Rust is the only other color in the kitchen. The steel sinks are full of crusted grime and dark brown rings. The floor drains are an ongoing science experiment.

A single metal bowl is lurking on the dry storage shelves, out of place, without a home. Lydia sees her reflection in the bowl. It's warped. How fitting. She has dark hair and tired eyes. Her black slacks are covered with cat hair, and so is the hoodie hiding her white collared shirt. But her red bowtie is

sticking out. Lydia feels like a clown. The bowtie is sneering at

her. *Why are you still working catering gigs with that expensive*

degree? She wants to burn them both.

A loud crash echoes across the kitchen. Lydia turns to

the noise. It's just an ice machine, doing what it does best, in the

loudest possible way. It's the size of an old arcade game. Lydia

can't believe it's still making ice. She doesn't want to know what

its creations look like. It's rude, hostile interruption is a

reminder. Lydia's inner alarm bells are blaring. Everyone who

works in the service industry has them. She's been here too long.

She needs to get back to the floor. A five minute disappearance

can be explained away. Lydia is pushing ten.

She shoves the fridge's metal door. Without that extra

push, it'll stay cracked open and leak cold air. It won't muffle

sound either. Lydia had to pull the door shut to scream in there.

Sealing yourself in a walk-in is always ominous, but that coffin

felt even more Siberian than it is outside. Lydia sees a

screwdriver on a shelf by the door. It's a perfect fit for a little

hole in the metal latch. Putting the screwdriver in there would seal the fridge. Lydia shudders. She forgot her phone. If she got locked in that cold metal box, she would've been fucked. Her cheeks are burning from the frost. At least she remembered her hoodie.

Lydia starts heading down a long hallway that leads back to the event. A glowing red exit sign at the end of the hall is the only color breaking up the grey monotony. The catering event Lydia found herself at tonight is in some old University hall. It's a busy shift. There are hundreds of guests and dozens of mercenaries like Lydia prowling a floor that's decorated like a Tsarist ballroom. At least, the parts that the public is supposed to see. The building itself is an opulent relic from upper-crust Nineteenth Century Boston. It's a place where robber barons came to get *culture,* and pretend that their hearts weren't blackened chunks of coal. Not much has changed.

There's a circular mirror coming up at the end of the hall. Lydia calls it the corner mirror. It's supposed to help busy workers see each other coming and avoid collisions at intersections like this one, but it rarely works out like that. Nothing does.

Lydia wasn't planning on screaming in an abandoned walk-in tonight, but then a drunk that looked like her doctor cornered her when she was carrying a tray of martinis. He was trying to get her number, and wouldn't let her move. Lydia could've given him the rejection hotline's digits, but she let go of her tray of drinks instead. The crash was loud. The hall got quiet. Broken glass and spilled liquor were everywhere, but most of it landed on the creep. He started crying about his ruined suit. Lydia ran to *go get her manager* and went to a forgotten walk-in to scream.

It almost worked. Lydia's hands stopped shaking. She's seeing colors other than red. The walk-in's free therapy has kept her from exploding on the job so far, but life is full of surprises.

Lydia just has to take a right at the corner mirror, then open a door halfway down the next corridor, and she'll be back on the floor. Then a door slams up ahead.

"Don't you see it, Bill? We can eradicate evil! Wipe it off the face of the earth! And you're trying to censor me! You're trying to bury this gift!"

Lydia freezes in place. What the fuck? Another voice yells.

"There you go again, Scott! Practicing *all* your future talking points, huh?"

"And just what is *that* supposed to mean, Bill?!?"

The shouting is getting louder. Two men are stomping down the hallway. They're heading right for Lydia. *Eradicating evil?* What the hell are they talking about? They're either really high, or they aren't in the industry. Lydia almost yells *CORNER*, but stares at the curved mirror instead. Men in suits are coming around the bend. Only scumbags like Lydia are supposed to be in this area, but these *respectable* men ignored the STAFF ONLY signs and came here.

For what? Privacy? Part of Lydia wants to stand her ground. They're invading her territory, her forgotten shit hole. She should tell them to get the fuck out of here, but she's wearing a hoodie full of cat hair. It doesn't look like she works here either.

Lydia walks backwards, slow and quiet. She pulls the walk-in's metal latch, gets back in the fridge, but doesn't pull the door all the way shut. She wants to listen and get a closer look. Lydia loves hearing petty fights between *respectable* people with *real* jobs. Humans are humans, no matter what costumes or titles they flaunt, and it's nice to know that the rich ones aren't happy either. Lydia's breath looks like smoke, but she peeks through the crack in the door.

Two men barge into the abandoned kitchen.

They both have glasses, arrogant demeanors and expensive suits. Neither of them look comfortable in suits, so they can't be lawyers. Lab coats must be their professional skin. They're both middle-aged, but time has been suspended for them in very different ways. One of them is toned and fit, and the other is chubby and pale. The fit man is bald, with big eyes and a trimmed goatee. The chubby guy has pink skin, beady, evasive eyes and curly blonde hair that makes him seem young in all the wrong ways. He's clutching a briefcase close to his chest.

Lydia knows him. She can't believe her *luck*. It's the same creep who hit on her earlier. He's the reason why she came to this forgotten corner of the kitchen to scream in the first place. The creep must be Scott, and the hot one must be Bill. Lydia shivers. Her thin hoodie isn't doing much about the cold. What the fuck is she doing? She doesn't have to hide, or deal with this shit. They're in the wrong, not her. Lydia is ready to startle them both, but then Bill says.

"I'm not denying that your project has noble intentions, Scott. I agree. It is *explosive* and *revolutionary*. That's precisely what's wrong with it."

Scott adjusts his glasses, pretends to look concerned and asks.

"What do you mean, Bill?"

"How many revolutions are peaceful, Scott?"

The two men stop by the dry storage shelves. Scott frowns and says.

"I see what you're getting at…"

"I don't think that you do, Scott! I don't think you're listening to me at all!"

Bill snatches the briefcase away from Scott. The creep yells.

"What the fuck!?!"

"I'm going to hold onto this briefcase and your precious little chips until you listen to me! If you actually do, you'll thank me one day. And if you don't, well, you'll wish that you did."

Scott backs up with his hands raised defensively, but he's looking for something in the kitchen, probably a weapon. The gloves are coming off now. Lydia is rooting for the hot one. What's in the briefcase? Who are they? Bill shouts.

"I think your ideas are dangerous, Scott. Even more dangerous than splitting the atom!"

"Come on, Bill! How *dare* you compare me to Oppenheimer! I'm not building nukes, or even making weapons! I'm doing the opposite! I'm eradicating evil from people's brains!"

Lydia reaches for her phone again, and curses herself for leaving it in her bag. Bill says.

"Oppenheimer couldn't imagine the implications of what he did, but he tried! You won't even do that! You're surrounded by yes-men, and you're all pretending that the chip's downsides don't exist, all so someone out there will write you a nice, big check tonight. Isn't that right?"

Scott grins and says.

"I think you're just jealous because no one says yes to any of *your* ideas, Bill."

If Lydia was Bill, she'd hit Scott. He's ripped enough to really make it count. Bill wants to knock the little shit out, but instead he holds up the briefcase and says.

"No one has said yes to this one either. I know that despite your swagger, you're broke. Your suit is rented. So is your car. You put this whole grotesque gala on credit, hoping to attract deep pockets to dig you out of this hole. I tried to warn you, and you fired me, remember?"

Scott smirks like an arrogant kid who knows that his dad rigged the big game. Lydia shivers. Her teeth are chattering. She hopes her manager forgot about her. If not, she can always blame sudden, explosive diarrhea. *No one* wants a follow-up to that story. Bill keeps talking.

"So, you *found* the part of our brains that controls morality. The proverbial fork in the road between good and evil. Your procedure, along with these implanted chips, will cut the link to the evil path, thus *curing* evil. Am I right so far?"

Scott nods. He'll listen to someone else, if they're talking about him. Bill goes on.

"You believe that with your chip, *evil* itself can be blocked. You think murderers can be made incapable of killing. But have you even *considered* the unintended consequences?"

Scott waves his arms dismissively and barks.

"Yes, yes, yes, of course! We've done dozens of trials, the procedure is harmless!"

Bill replies like a lawyer who's one question away from having no further questions.

"*Harmless,* interesting choice of word. And it was twenty trials, to be exact. We know your chip works, what comes next? You spent a lot of time making the procedure possible, and profitable; but you didn't spend any time pondering the nature of evil, morality, or humanity."

"What the fuck is *that* supposed to mean, Bill?!?"

"Your chip is going to rewire human brains, to make them more *moral*, but you don't even know *what* morality is. And you clearly haven't spent *any* time studying evil either. Hell, you didn't even study Subject Twenty. You remember what happened to that poor bastard, don't you, Scott? Or, I should say, that poor bastard's family."

"I don't know what you're talking about. There were only nineteen subjects."

Scott's reply sounded practiced. This is touchy subject for him. Bill laughs, then says.

"You're lying. I know about Subject Twenty, and I know about that little favor you had to call in with your friends in the military to make him, and any records of him, disappear. How did it feel to cover up the brutal murder of an innocent woman and a child? Tell me, Scott, did you look at those crime scene photos before you hit delete?"

"I don't have time for this. The presentation is about to start. Give me that briefcase!"

Scott moves to snatch the bag, but Bill pushes him against the wall and shouts.

"*Make* time!"

Scott struggles. He wants to call for help, but he's too scared. He's clearly never been threatened before. His entitled sense of security is eroding fast. Something crashes in the kitchen. Both men jump and turn to the noise. It's just the ice machine making more ice. Bill looks around the kitchen. Lydia is glad she went back into the walk-in, but then Bill looks right at her. Her heart stops, then he looks away. Did he see her? Maybe not. Bill grabs Scott and says.

"Let's go into that walk-in to finish our conversation. Someone might be listening."

Lydia panics all over again. She darts her head around the fridge. The cocoon of plastic bags and metal shelves around the cake is tall enough to hide her. There's a small clearing under the bagged partition. Lydia gets down on the cold metal floor and slides into the cocoon. When she stands up next to the cake, the walk-in opens. Bill drags Scott inside. The heavy door closes behind them, but not all the way. Bill pushes Scott against the cold wall, gets close and says.

"No one can hear us in here. Caterers go in here to shout and let off steam. I did the same thing when I had to work during school. Tell me Scott, did you work during college?"

"There you go again, Bill. You've always been a *dedicated* class warrior, haven't you? Always using your *hard* upbringing as an excuse. Well, at *MIT*, we didn't have time to…"

Bill slaps Scott across the face and shouts.

"What was that?!?"

Scott looks like he just shit himself. He says nothing. Bill smirks, then says.

"You probably think I'm being evil right now, don't you?"

Scott nods. His eyes are glittering with hate. Bill says.

"Well, *I* don't think I'm being evil. Not at all. I think I'm doing more good than you can possibly imagine. I think I'm acting like a fucking angel, and I'm doing it for *your own good*!"

Scott grows pale when he sees that Bill means every word he's saying. Bill adds.

"You see, Scott, that's the tricky thing about us humans. We *all* think we're the good guys. You, me, and everyone else! Stalin? He thought he was leading hundreds of millions of people to a utopian paradise! And if millions had to die for that *greater good,* who cares, *right*?"

Scott says nothing. He's terrified, and Bill has his undivided attention. Lydia shivers and tries to hide the noise from her chattering teeth. How long has she been in here? She almost bumps into the cake on a rolling platter behind her. Bill says.

"Did slave owners think they were evil? Not at all! They thought the Bible told them it was okay! Hell, we even call some of them Founding Fathers now."

Scott is squirming. He doesn't want a history lesson. He wants to get the briefcase and get the fuck out of here, but without authority figures to get his way, he can't. Bill keeps talking.

"Are you beginning to see a pattern here, Scott?"

Scott says nothing, but he's breathing fast. It looks like he's chain smoking. Bill says.

"What *is* morality? You think it's built into all of us, that every new baby has a clear moral code that falls apart upon contact with the world. But you have it backwards. Morality is given to us *by* the world, by society, by our family, our friends, even our enemies. Surgically removing the path to the *evil* part of our brain sounds nice, on paper. It's an easy thing to sponsor too. But if you actually think this will *cure* evil, it will backfire in ways you can't even imagine."

Scott opens his mouth to interject, but Bill keeps talking.

"*You* think I'm being evil, but for me, not trying to stop you is evil. In my mind, stopping your project is the greatest good there is. If the *evil* path of my brain was closed, if there was no balance, no need to debate, if I couldn't *help* but do good, I wouldn't try to convince you. I'd just kill you. *That* would stop your project far more effectively than this fucking speech, don't you think? For me, killing you wouldn't be evil at all, it'd serve the greater good. A real win-win."

Scott turns as pale as ivory. Bill goes on.

"You think you're going to create a world of angels with your chip, but you're only going to make more devils. Subject Twenty thought he was being merciful when he killed his family. During his psych evals, he told us that he was conflicted about raising a kid in this world, seeing the way that it's headed. So in his mind, after he got the chip, murdering his family spared them from far worse horrors in the future. Don't you see? Your procedure *worked* on Subject Twenty, better than anyone else! He thought he was being a good guy, and nothing stopped him!"

Bill shakes the briefcase in front of Scott's face and shouts.

"All because of your chip! From what I hear, even from the hole in the ground that your military friends threw him in, Subject Twenty *still* has no regrets! He's going to die thinking he was a hero who saved his family. He should've made you halt this project then, but instead you buried his results and focused on the simple, optimistic, comfortable people from your earlier trials and kept chugging along. None of them did anything bad, but that's what they always did."

Bill shakes his head, shoves the briefcase into Scott's chest and says.

"But I know that you won't listen to a word I say, so take it! It's your bomb, not mine. I said my piece. I don't have the chip yet, so I'm done trying to stop you. Go on, get to your *big* speech! But when you're telling all the dignified people in that ballroom about your *explosive, revolutionary* chip, just remember what explosions and revolutions actually look like."

Bill turns away from Scott in disgust. Scott grins. He already forgot everything Bill said. Lydia's heart is thudding. She's stunned by all the things she just heard. She doesn't know what she's going to do. Scott is anxious to return to the warm, bright and comfortable world where he belongs. Bill starts walking towards the door, but it opens before he can get to it.

Someone else is coming in to join the party.

A man with shiny medals and a crisp, olive green military uniform walks into the fridge. He's clapping. Lydia stops breathing altogether. Bill and Scott are frozen, staring at the military man with eyes full of terror. He has a severe, hawk-like face and short silver hair. Command comes naturally for him. He's used to it. He was born to do it. He must be a general. He barks.

"Now *that* was a fascinating discussion!"

The heavy door closes behind the general, but not all the way. No one replies, so he adds.

"What? You *smart guys* left the door cracked open, so I waited outside and heard it all!"

The general's glare is sharp, cold and hyper-vigilant. Heavy bags under his eyes say he's always alert. The scientists won't say his name out loud. Lydia can't read his nametag either. It's a hell of a way to find out she needs glasses. The general approaches Bill and says.

"I have to commend you, Bill. I've sat with people more powerful than you can possibly imagine, and you have a far better grasp of the true nature of evil and morality than any of them. I want to hear more."

Bill nods, real slow. Both he and Scott are terrified. They know the general. His medals reflect the ugly fluorescents above. Is he the *friend* that Bill was talking about? The one who hid Subject Twenty for Scott? He was listening to them from the shadows, just like Lydia. Bill says.

"I'm flattered."

He's calm. Bill has dealt with dangerous men with authority all his life. The general says.

"That's good. Very good. I recorded the whole thing, but I'd like you to repeat it again, in person, for the Joint Chiefs of Staff. How does that sound, Bill?"

Scott is jealous. He looks like a boiling pink tea pot that's about to burst. He shouts.

"Hey! Does this mean you're going to sponsor *my* project or what?!?"

Silence descends upon the cold metal box. Scott is still holding the briefcase.

He shouts like a small, raving dog, desperate to assert its worth. Scott probably had to summon all the courage in his wet noodle of a soul to do it. All the humor vanishes from the general's face. He's the kind of man who can send thousands to die with the same emotional detachment that Lydia uses to pick up a big tray full of expensive drinks. The general turns to Scott. The creep cowers like a bad dog, but then the general starts laughing. It bursts out of him. Frozen mist and spit fly out of his mouth. The general slaps his knee, then shouts.

"*Sponsor* it? Hell, I'm taking it over!"

Scott's eyes light up. He starts laughing too. The general says.

"I don't know why *you're* laughing, Scott. You're no longer in charge of this project."

Scott looks like he just got the death penalty. He legs get wobbly. He stammers.

"But...what...how..."

"You were about to present your chip to the world. That's not going to happen. It's only useful for us if no one knows about it. It's now the property of the Pentagon. From now on, it'll be supervised by more capable hands, by someone who understands what you created."

The general glares at Scott, begging him to say something different. Scott gets quiet. He's still holding onto the briefcase, but it looks like he's sinking into a deep, dark place. Fear is growing in Bill's eyes too. The general grins and goes on.

"Don't worry, Scott. You're a carpenter who accidentally raised a piano prodigy. Do you think it should be taught by a carpenter, or by another pianist, someone who understands their gift in ways that you never can? Don't be upset, your creation surpassed you! And if you're worried about money, well, that's *never* a problem for my people."

The general turns to Bill and goes on.

"But when it comes to running this project, Bill, I think you're perfect for the job."

Horror, joy, hate, confusion, rage, dread and resignation all wash over Bill's face. He doesn't know what to say. The general is grinning like a wolf. Lydia's heart is thundering. She's witnessing genuine history. The kind of stuff that transcends the front page and the trending bar on social media. The kind of history that Lydia's grandchildren will argue about. It's all happening right here, and she's the only person around who has any incentive to tell the world about it. She has to get out of here. She has to tell somebody, anybody. But she left her phone in her backpack. What will Bill do? Take the job? Lydia backs up, then Bill shouts.

"I'm not letting *either* of you take this fucking thing out of here!"

Bill shoves Scott into the metal shelves. It's a loud crash. Trays and food fly. Scott gets buried in food that went bad long ago. Bill snatches the briefcase from him and charges at the general. The fight doesn't last long. The general dodges Bill and gets him in a chokehold. While Bill struggles, the general pulls a metal baseball out of his pocket. Scott looks relieved. He thinks he's been saved, but Lydia knows better. The general's eyes are glazed over. He isn't going to be done killing until he's the last man standing in here.

Lydia's chest is pounding. Is someone looking for her? She doubts it. They all came to this part of the kitchen for the same reason. No one else is coming. An unfortunate realization is dawning on Lydia. She's going to have to do something. The general says.

"In that case, I'm taking this to the Pentagon by myself. We have no further use for either of you, but don't worry, I'll know the *heroic* sacrifice you both made for our national security."

The general pulls a pill out of the metal baseball. It starts glowing. He says.

"The gas will start coming out in five seconds. Relax, and the end will come peacefully."

The general drops the baseball. Lydia reacts without thinking. She yells.

"CORNER!!!"

And runs through the plastic bags like a ribbon at the end of a marathon. Lydia charges at the general and shoulder checks him. He tries to grab her as he falls down, but winds up with a handful of plastic instead. He crashes into metal shelves and lands on top of Scott. Lydia hears something heavy hit the floor. She grabs Bill by his sportscoat and yells.

"C'MON! LET'S GO!!"

Bill bolts up and runs out of the walk-in with Lydia. He's startled. He has the briefcase and a lot of questions, but Lydia rams the fridge's metal door with her shoulder before he can ask them. Bill gets next to her and helps. As the door is closing, Lydia sees Scott staring at her. He's begging for mercy, then starts to recognize her from earlier. How fitting.

When the door shuts, Bill starts to relax, but then a charging bull crashes into it from the other side. Lydia and Bill brace the door with all of their weight. How many seconds has it been?

Then Lydia sees the screwdriver.

It's still sitting on the same shelf, right next to the walk-in. She shoves it into the hole in the door latch. Bill and Lydia step back. The door keeps thudding from the bull on the other side, but it doesn't budge. Then the thuds start to lose their intensity. It's been more than five seconds since the general dropped the strange metal baseball in there. Lydia doesn't hear any screaming, or any other noises coming from inside the fridge. That's the beautiful part about walk-ins.

Bill turns to Lydia in the dirty kitchen. He's still holding the briefcase. His eyes are wide and startled. His mouth opens to ask her a barrage of stupid questions, but Lydia shouts first.

"No time, we have to get the fuck out of here!"

Lydia runs down the hall. Now she's happy that she forgot her phone. Bill follows behind her. He doesn't have a choice. Lydia takes a left at the corner mirror and kicks an emergency exit door open in the next corridor. Lydia and Bill run out into the cold, winter night.

MARK

A screeching printer startles Dave. The harsh clanging echoes across the warehouse. It's huge. There are no walls in here. Endless, tall aisles full of entertainment products divide it into sections. Dave works alone, in a forgotten corner full of DVDs. He just got his first order of the day. Someone wants a Rachel Ray cooking DVD. It's a holiday special. Why? Why not?

Dave heads for the R shelf. The trip is long and lonely. He passes aisles full of dusty, shrink-wrapped movies. A lot of people worked in this section once, but no one buys DVDs anymore. Everyone else was laid off, or sent to other departments, but Dave outlasted them all.

Now he's all alone in here, with the concrete, metal, cinderblocks and plastic. Dave reaches the R shelf and starts hunting. He sees *Rambo*, *Raising Arizona*, *That's so Raven*, *Red Dragon*, *Robin Hood: Men in Tights*, *Run Lola Run*, but no Rachel Ray. Where is she?

Fuck. Dave walks all the way back to the computer and types. The old system says that Rachel's special is in stock, but the *where* section was never filled in. Dave surveys his dusty kingdom. Shit. It's a free-for-all down here. No one is around. No one cares about DVDs.

Dave could always ask Mark, but Mark doesn't talk much.

Patty *could* help, but her office is at the other end of the warehouse. Dave will have to walk past the comics, the CDs, and the toys. Sections with workers, who aren't obsolete like Dave and his DVDs. Hell, even the vinyl guy is popular again. Patty runs this whole warehouse, and if she has to walk all the way over here to find Dave's only order of the day, he'll be fucked.

That can't happen. Dave will have to find Rachel by himself, and fast. The warehouse is about to close. The last delivery trucks are going out in twenty minutes. But what can he do?

The vast, chaotic section is taunting him. A random, lost DVD could be hiding anywhere. Dave doesn't know where to start. He looks at the crawling conveyor belt that snakes around the building. This moving sidewalk feeds boxes up to the delivery trucks outside. He could jump on, ride it all the way to the top, scare the stoned guys at the other end and get the fuck out of here, but Dave wants to keep his strange professional existence. It's the only one he's ever known.

Why hasn't Patty fired Dave already? Does she need someone to pick on? Maybe she's lonely. Running this whole warehouse must be hard. Dave is terrified of her, but also in love. Patty looks like Isabella Rossellini in *Wild at Heart*. She's ageless and fierce, with wise, piercing eyes. Her hair always changes, but she's never been seen without a leather jacket. Patty wears a lot of rings, but they look more like weapons than decorations. Her fiery temper makes sense. All the workers in the other sections are assholes. Running this shit-show must be exhausting.

Patty asked Dave about random movies in the past, but he always fled. Maybe it wasn't a trap. Maybe he should've talked to her. They're about the same age. Maybe Patty wants a date. Dave shakes his head. That's how things work in movies, not in the warehouse where they're stored. Dave has to find this rogue DVD, but he doesn't have time to scan every aisle.

Where else can he look?

Dave turns to the sagging pile of boxes next to the conveyor belt. Its summit is taller than him. Its jagged, cratered, chaotic shape looks like a tense Jenga game that never got finished. The pile seemed like it was about to topple over on Dave's first day, but it's held firm ever since.

A deadhead named George who worked in this section long ago called it *box mountain*. He said that every weird, missing DVD is hiding in there. Long ago, some dickhead scanned a shit-ton of product into the warehouse, piled it all up into this cardboard summit, and quit. No one knows why he did it, but now, years later, Dave will have to search box mountain.

Where to begin? Dave has to be careful. The pile of old, stained cardboard is stacked in a way that'd give the creators of Tetris some fucked up nightmares. Pulling the wrong piece could destabilize box mountain. If it topples over, the avalanche could crush the conveyor belt and shut down the whole warehouse. That would be bad. Real bad. But the clock is also ticking. Shit.

Dave coughs up dust and wipes sweat off his forehead.
Some boxes have markings. They say *Q*, *MISC BULLSHIT*, and
ABANDON ALL HOPE YE WHO ENTER HERE. Most are
blank. Rachel could be hiding in any of them. Dave only has one
option left. He'll have to ask Mark.

Dave looks below the conveyor belt. His old friend is
still there. The dead mouse is surrounded by spider webs and
clumps of dust. He's well-preserved, which is strange, because
this mouse has been rotting down here for at least ten years. A
handwritten card on a metal placeholder next to him reads RIP
MARK. Dave bows his head, clears his throat and says.

"Hi, Mark. You don't happen to know which box Rachel
Ray is hiding in, do you?"

Mark says nothing. It isn't surprising. He never talks.
He's Dave's favorite coworker. Why hasn't time reduced this
mouse to a skeleton? Bugs should've picked him dry by now, but
maybe this large, dusty warehouse is so devoid of life that even
bugs want nothing to do with it.

Dave looks up. A box that says *RUN* looks promising.
Did someone try to alphabetize this chaos? Maybe. He pulls at

RUN. It gives, then the soggy cardboard gets stuck. Box mountain starts leaning. Uh-oh. Dave should heed this warning, but the last truck goes out in ten minutes.

Fuck it. He pulls as hard as he can. Something tears. The *RUN* box slides out fast, almost as if it was shoved. It's heavy. Dave staggers back, slips, and lands on his ass. Pain shocks his tailbone like a cattle prod. He looks up. Box mountain is tilting forward, in a terminal decline. Gravity is all the momentum it needs. Dave runs for the conveyor belt. If this moving road gets crushed, he'd rather go out with it than live to face Patty's wrath.

Hell, maybe Dave and Mark will finally have something to talk about.

But gravity gives him a break. Box mountain is falling the other way. Dave watches it come down like a big tree in the woods. The impact echoes across the warehouse. A wave of dust washes over Dave. He sneezes when it clears up. Ripped boxes and products are spilled out all over the floor. It doesn't look like box mountain fell over. It's like it got hit by a grenade.

The vertical pile of chaos is now horizontal, but the conveyer belt was spared. Dave sees bobble head toys, records and a *Fringe* DVD boxed-set among the debris. It's the last

season. Dave smiles. He liked that show, but never finished it.

He shakes his head. Box mountain fell on the spot where he was

standing. He should've stayed put. Now he has to deal with this

mess.

Dave only has five minutes before the last truck goes

out. The *RUN* box is his last hope. The cardboard flaps are sealed

with ancient, peeling tape. Dave rips it open. He blinks. Holy

shit.

The box is full of Rachel Ray DVDs.

Dave finds the holiday special that started this mess. He

got lucky. He wants to know more about the person who ordered

this DVD in the middle of July, until he sees something shiny in

the middle of the box full of Rachels. It's a golden cube.

It's shaped like a cigar box, but it's ornate, and full of

small carvings. The golden cube looks like a spoiled monarch's

jewelry case. It could be historic. It doesn't have a barcode

either. The shiny case is surrounded by a dozen Rachels, as if her

clones are guards. What's in there? The devil on Dave's shoulder

tells him to look. So does his angel. Then a new voice pipes up.

"You don't want to open that, Dave."

Dave screams. Who the fuck was that? The voice sounded gravelly, like an old smoker. Dave darts his head around and scans his lifeless corner of the warehouse, but he doesn't see a newly retired garbage truck driver down here, or anyone else. He yells.

"Who's there?!?"

"Who else, Einstein? It's me, Mark!"

Dave shudders. It can't be. He crouches down and looks at the long dead mouse.

"I'm still here, jackass! The last truck is leaving in two minutes, so throw that fucking Rachel Ray DVD on the conveyor belt before we *both* get shit-canned!"

Dave is stunned, but Mark is right, even if he's mysteriously exempt from decomposition. Dave puts the holiday special on the conveyor belt. Rachel crawls towards the trucks upstairs. She doesn't have a sticker or a box, but if the drivers are confused by that lone DVD, they can fucking call it in. Dave doesn't care. He looks at the golden cube. It has tiny, intricate designs, like carvings on columns in ancient auditoriums. What the hell is this thing? Mark says.

"Trust me, Dave. Don't open that. Don't even look at it. Put it down."

Fuck it. Dave doesn't care how crazy he might sound. He replies to the phantom mouse.

"Why, Mark? Do *you* know what's in there?"

"As a matter of fact, I do. I've been here a *lot* longer than you, tiger. I saw the guy who made box mountain, the *agent of chaos,* as you call him."

Dave stares at the dead mouse. Its little mouth isn't moving, but somehow it can talk, and read his thoughts too. Dave ignores the obvious insanity all around, plays along and says.

"So what, did he tell *you* what this thing does?"

"No, Dave. I'm a fucking mouse. But I saw him. He was a ruined man. He was talking to the cube. He cursed it. He said he'd bury it where no one could find it. And here we are."

Mark laughs like nothing is funny. It echoes across the warehouse. Dave says.

"What's wrong with it, Mark? Does this box get you really fucking high or something?"

"Even worse than that, Dave. It grants one wish."

The mouse stops laughing. A fly is buzzing in the distance. Dave says.

"What, like a fucking genie or something?"

"Call it whatever you want, Dave, just don't fucking open it!"

Dave blinks. Really? Maybe Mark isn't joking. One wish? Dave looks at the shiny case with new eyes. It's still surrounded by Rachels in its soggy cardboard tomb. They're getting heavy, and Dave's greed is running in overdrive. He sets the box down on the floor and says.

"Why should I listen to you, Mark? Are you my boss now?"

"You wish, Dave. I'm just trying to do you a favor."

Dave keeps staring at the golden cube. Is it really a genie? He thinks about his tiny, shithole apartment, his roommates, his debts, his bills. With the right wish, they could all go away. But he's thinking small. Dave can make his dreams come true. But what are they? He stopped chasing them long ago. Did he forgot what they were? It looks so easy. Mark says.

"Don't do it, Dave."

Dave's frustration boils over. He turns to the mouse under the conveyer belt and shouts.

"Why shouldn't I make a wish? My life is shit, and I found this fucking thing!"

"Have you ever heard of the term *unintended consequences*?"

"Of course I have! What do you think I am, Mark? An idiot?"

"Well, you *do* work in the DVD sec…"

"Shut up and let me think!"

Dave feels guilty after saying that. Mark is his only friend. He says.

"I'm sorry, man. That was…"

"I don't want apologies, Dave! I want you to listen to me! *Any* wish will fuck you over!"

Dave nods, but he's still trying to think of a shortcut. Mark sighs and keeps talking.

"You need examples? Fine. I bet you want a lot of money, don't you?"

"Of course I do, Mark! Who doesn't?"

"*I* don't, but that's not important right now. If you open that cube and wish for a million dollars, robbers will come for it. They'll have suits and briefcases, or masks and guns."

Dave wants to ask about a billion out of spite, but he thinks out loud instead.

"A girlfriend would be nice…"

"Jeez, what could go wrong with that? She could be a serial killer, a con artist, a…"

"I get it, you fucking asshole!"

"Do you? Let me tell you something, Dave. Things can *always* get worse!"

Dave frowns. He's letting a dead mouse tell him what to do. How is Mark even talking? Is this a prank? Dave looks around. Lights flicker above. Distant laughter echoes from the other side of the warehouse, but his forgotten corner is quiet. It's just Dave, Mark, and dusty DVDs. No one is coming, even after box mountain fell over. Maybe it didn't. Maybe Dave finally lost it. Or maybe the best part of his life is about to begin. Dave picks up the golden cube.

It crackles in his fingers. Shit. Mark might be a hallucination, but Dave feels electricity churning through the golden cube. He inspects it like a TSA agent. He finds hinges, and a lid with no lock. He wants to open it. It'll be easy. But if Mark is fake, who's talking? Is it the cube? Does it want to be alone? Dave's greed keeps looking for a wish without side effects. He says.

"I could wish for a different job. *Anything* would be better than this!"

"Are you even listening to yourself? *Anything*? Really? Ever work in a slaughterhouse, Dave? How about a prison? Ever gone to war? Fuck out of here! *At least* half of humanity would kill for your life, you just can't imagine something worse, because you've always had it so good! You think you *deserve* better, but are too dull and spoiled to even know what you want!"

Dave blinks. That stung, mostly because Mark is right. What did Dave want to be? He's always loved movies, hasn't he? Didn't Dave want to make them? Or did he want to be an actor?

Shit. Dave can't remember. He scours his brain like he got a new order, but his memory files are a clusterfuck maze, even worse than this warehouse. He hunts for old hopes and dreams, but Dave finds a car accident. Hospitals. Funerals. He buried those memories to survive, but his dreams and aspirations must've been entombed along with them, if they even existed. Mark says.

"Please, Dave. Listen to me. Put that golden cube back in the box and burn it."

Dave looks between the shiny box and the dead mouse. Maybe *Mark* is the trick here, the test that Dave has to pass before he can unleash the power that he found. He says.

"Tell me something, Mark. How do you know so much about this golden cube?"

Dave holds it closer to his chest. Its inner, crackling charge rattles his ribs. Mark sighs.

"Look at the corner of the box that you found it in."

Dave squints between two Rachel Ray DVDs and sees a chewed out hole. Mark says.

"That's how I got in there. I was a lot like you, Dave. I loved this place, because it's safe. Other mice hate this warehouse, so I could be alone here. But Patty hates *rodents*. Her porters hunt for food scraps like they're keeping bears away, and they lock up that dumpster outside like Fort Knox. I was always hungry in here, but I never wanted to leave. So I saw opportunity in the agent of chaos. He looked haunted, aged beyond his years, like he got everything he wanted; all at once and far too soon. Somehow, I knew that his golden cube could stop the hunger. I climbed box mountain and dug around until I found it, just like you. That's when I heard Walter."

The golden cube is buzzing now, hard, almost angrily. Mark keeps talking.

"Walter warned me not to open it, but my stomach was growling too loud to listen to the fly. I had one wish in mind, and one wish alone. I wished to never be hungry again."

Dave gulps, and looks at the long dead mouse, covered in dust bunnies, spider webs and with his own handwritten tombstone mounted on a rusted placeholder. Mark says.

"I got my wish. You're looking at it."

Dave is dizzy. The golden cube is getting heavier the longer he holds it. It's buzzing like an angry insect, but the carvings on this shiny case are forming a smile. Is he tripping? Dave looks closer. The grin is a mosaic. It's made of a thousand scowling demons.

Shit. Dave should listen to Mark, but his greed is screaming. It needs to make a wish.

Dave can think of something better. He's smarter than a rodent and an insect. Isn't he?

Thunder rumbles outside. Dave itches his head, then a long lost memory jumps out, clear as day. He knows his wish. Dave used it when he was a kid, on a trip to a children's museum. No one tried it out in cartoons, or even in the *Twilight Zone*. Yes. Dave's wish seems logical, safe, and full of wondrous potential. He can't see any downsides either. He grins, then says.

"I have my wish, Mark. *Nothing* can possibly go wrong with this!"

The golden cube feels nice, light and warm again. Maybe Dave solved the ancient riddle.

"Don't do it, you crazy bastard!"

Fucking Mark. Dave scowls at the dead mouse under the conveyer belt and shouts.

"How do I know that *you* aren't part of the golden cube? Huh?!"

"*I am,* you jackass! So is Walter, the fly. Our souls are trapped in here. You want the truth? I'm not doing this because we like you, Dave. Walter and I just *really* don't want to spend eternity with you! So at least do us a favor and tell us about your supposed *fool-proof* wish!"

Dave is offended and relieved at the same time, but he's mostly angry, so he talks shit.

"Wait, mice and flies have souls?"

"Who the hell do you think you've been talking to? Tell us your wish, you damn moron!"

"But won't that make it happen?"

"Not if you say it before opening that fucking cube! God, you *really* are dense, Dave!"

Dave can't let a dead mouse talk to him like this, but he decides to out-class it. He says.

"Fine, Mark. I'm going to wish for World Peace!"

For a second, the warehouse gets quiet. Dave thinks he won, until Mark starts laughing. It's loud and wheezy. Even his coughs sound celebratory. Dave tightens his grip around the golden cube. His cheeks flush. He hates being laughed at. Mark yells.

"Really, Dave? REALLY?!? You don't think *anything* could go wrong with that one?"

Dave sees red. He's about to explode, but then he hears a new noise. It's a faint buzzing, but fast moving and staccato. In and out, like it's breathing. Dave has never heard a fly laugh before, but this one sounds like it's rolling on the floor. Is it the fly that Mark was talking about? Fuck him. Dave wants to throw the golden cube at the dead mouse, but he yells instead.

"What!? Tell me, what could go wrong with World Peace? It's what everyone wants!"

The fly and the mouse stop laughing. The warehouse gets quiet. The last trucks went out a long time ago. Distant lights shut off. Uh-oh. Dave doesn't want to get locked in. Mark says.

"That might be the most dangerous wish I've ever heard. You didn't think about what World Peace means, did you? From what? War? You didn't specify. Conflict is part of life, Dave. Just try and eat without it. Peace sounds great, but no one wants the kind of peace that the golden cube will bring. It'll be nuclear winter, my guy! You'll make your wish, and wake up in a fucking blizzard of ash! Grey, permanent ash. Nothing will move, nothing will stir, and as far as you'll see, the world will be at peace. Is that what you want, Dave?"

Dave gulps. He looks down at the golden cube with horror. He can see it all, clear as day. He doesn't want to admit he was wrong, but he doesn't want that grey blizzard either. Dave says.

"No."

"Thank fuck. Here's a free tip. Instead of crying about how *shitty* your life is, Dave, try being grateful. You ever stop to listen to the fucking birds, man? You ever just sit in the sunlight, shut your eyes and smile? Of course not, you people have their heads drilled too far up your own asses to appreciate the little things. If you need to change your life, quit waiting for magical shit like the cube to do it for you. Just fucking do it! And if you can't, then do us all a big favor and quit fucking complaining! But whatever you do, do *not* open that damn cube! *BURN IT*!!!"

Mark is right. Dave shuts his eyes, smothers his inner greed, then says.

"You're right, Mark. Fuck this thing. I *will* burn it!"

"WHAT THE FUCK ARE YOU TALKING ABOUT, DAVE?!?"

Dave yelps like a dog and jumps. He knows the voice behind him. Patty keeps shouting.

"WHAT ARE YOU GOING TO BURN!?! WHO ARE YOU TALKING TO!?! LOOK AT ME, GODDAMNIT!!!"

Dave turns around. Patty is right behind him. He almost gets the rush of joy and fear that only a crush can provide, but now it's just terror. Patty's eyes are bloodshot and shaking in their sockets. Her fists are clenched, white with tension. She's fucking furious. Dave stammers.

"Hello…Patty. How…"

"WHAT ARE YOU GOING TO…"

Patty looks down and cuts herself off. She was furious a second ago, but now she sees the golden cube. Her posture shifts. Her breathing slows. Her fists unclench. Patty says.

"What are you holding there, Dave?"

Before the angels, devils, mice and flies in his mind can start piping up, Dave gives Patty the golden cube. She cradles it and stares, with a mix of curiosity and greed. Dave says.

"I was looking for a Rachel Ray DVD, then box mountain came down. It almost crushed me! I could've died! But don't worry, Patty, the DVD is on the trucks. I found that weird, shiny case in the same box. There's no barcode. It looks valuable. *You* know what to do with it, right?"

Dave is pointing at the cardboard ruins behind him, but Patty doesn't look up. Dave says.

"Can I clock out and go home now? That last order almost killed me!"

"Yes, good idea. I'm happy you're alright, Dave. I was worried about you."

Patty smiles, but she doesn't look up from the golden cube. She's always sharp and alert, but now her eyes are lost and glazed. Is Mark talking to her? Dave looks under the conveyor belt.

The dead mouse is gone. Mark's body turned to dust and blew away, but his tombstone still stands. In the future, people will wonder who Mark was, and why someone left a tribute for him under the conveyor belt. Not Dave. By refusing to make a wish, he set Mark's soul free. He went where he was supposed to be long ago. Maybe Walter the fly went with him. But now Patty is holding their old prison. She's staring at the golden cube with the kind of greed it thrives on.

Dave should be worried, but from what he learned about the cube's strange brand of evil, only selfless wishes turn out bad for everyone else. Then Patty looks down and exclaims.

"Wait a minute! Is that the last season of *Fringe*?"

She drops the golden cube like a piece of trash. It makes a loud thud when it hits the floor, and pops open. What will happen now? The noise doesn't pry Patty's eyes away from the DVD. They're wide and full of wonder. Her mask is gone. Dave remembers his crush. He looks down, pretends to notice the *Fringe* boxed set for the first time and says.

"Wow! Holy shit, you like that show?"

Patty looks up at him skeptically, but his enthusiasm makes her smile. She says.

"Like? I fucking *love* that show!"

"Hell yeah! I do too!"

"I just never saw the last season…"

Dave blinks. This is too good to be true, but he rolls with it and says.

"Me neither!"

Patty frowns. Maybe she thinks this is too good to be true as well. She says.

"That weird sci-fi episode towards the end of season four confused the shit out of me."

"Same here! Walter woke up like a boss though. What he did to those Observers, man…"

Patty smiles. Light returns to her eyes. Dave just passed some kind of a test. She says.

"Fuck those bald assholes, and their fedoras too. You know, Dave, I have a pretty big TV at my house. If you don't have any plans after this, maybe we could watch it together…"

This can't be real. Then Dave hears a low, whistling noise below, like a boiling tea kettle. The golden cube is shaking. Uh-oh. Patty looks down and says.

"What the…"

Then the golden cube vanishes. It imploded on itself, like a microscopic vacuum just swallowed it whole. Patty blinks. So does Dave. He doesn't know what to say. She stammers.

"…Hell was that?"

A printer screeches close by. Patty and Dave yelp at the same time. They all echo across the warehouse. Dave just got his second order of the day. He looks above the aisles full of dusty products. A block of lights shut off in the distance. Maybe it was the toy section. It must get real lonely in here when it's dark. Dave is happy. Mark is free. He'll listen to the dead mouse's advice. He'll be grateful for what he has, and won't wait for a magic force to change his life, he'll do it himself. Starting now.

Dave winks at Patty, then says.

"How about I tell you when we start season five?"

ACKNOWLEDGEMENTS

First of all, I have to thank Mara Birkerts, my brilliant partner. She edited this whole damn book, minus this part, which is probably why it's so unreadable. She got me back into writing, and she gets me. I hope I get her too. She's gorgeous, and a joy to be around. She keeps it real, compulsively, and she's a steel-spined defender of the most marginalized and stigmatized people in society. In short, I'm *damn* lucky that we both swiped right.

Thank you to my mother, Christine Lund. She is a master poet, and a damn good writer too. She raised me to be the semi-decent human that I am today, and we helped steer each other through truly dark times, with art, jokes, and love. She read these stories before you, and helped me swat down the most ridiculous grammatical errors. I'm sure we didn't catch them all, but dammit, we tried. *"So it goes…"* As Vonnegut said. Thank you to Neil Trager, ace photographer, curator extraordinaire, master chef, and a wonderful step-father.

Thank you to Missy, who just nudged my leg, demanding a snack. Thank you to Joe, napping peacefully next to me as I write this now. Thank you to Buddy, Joni, Frankie, and all the other green giants that grace this apartment with their presence.

Thank you to my sister, Kaja. And thank you to my father, Bill. It's really hard to write this part. Losing you two almost destroyed me. But what y'all taught me while you were still here helped me survive. Thank you. I know you're watching me now, and I hope I'm only disappointing you a *little* bit.

Thank you to Jet Zarkadas and Jeff Lund, my godmother and godfather. They are both avid, lifelong readers, and a constant inspiration to me, so I have a sneaking suspicion that all of this might be their fault.

Thank you to Appolonia Vargas, my legendary band-mate. I'm sorry that my solo album turned into a book, I don't know what the hell happened. Ratchet By Nature will never die.

Thank you to all my other friends and family members who gave me life, and helped bring me to this point. Holy shit. There are so damn many of you. If I start trying to list y'all, I might fuck around and write a whole other book. Just know that I love you, and I'm sorry for everything. You know who you are. Thank you, from the bottom of my heart.

Thank you to Whomever It May Concern, upstairs.

BIOGRAPHY

Sam Mauldin was born in 1986, in Santa Fe, New Mexico. He now lives in Brooklyn, with his magical partner Mara, their lovely cats Joe and Missy, and a legion of giant rubber trees.

This is his first collection of short stories.

Before Times is a mix of horror, sci-fi, and magical realism, just like our modern world.